About the Author

William Mayne set out to write books at the age of eight, and about twenty years later won a Carnegie Medal.

Occasionally he gets the piano out and tries a bit of music writing. Much more often he bakes bread and eats that. Quite a lot of the time he is working out new computer programs for some local schools. Always he is waiting for new ideas for stories. But it is a long time since he was eight and knew how to do it easily.

He lives in a cottage in the Yorkshire Dales.

Midnight Fair

William Mayne

Hodder
Children's
Books

a division of Hodder Headline plc

Copyright © 1997 William Mayne

First published in hardback in Great Britain in 1997
by Hodder Children's Books

This paperback edition published in Great Britain in 1998
by Hodder Children's Books

The right of William Mayne to be identified as the Author
of the Work has been asserted by him in accordance with the
Copyright, Designs and Patents Act 1988.

10 9 8 7 6 5 4 3 2 1

A Catalogue record for this book is available
from the British Library

ISBN 0 340 65679 4

Typeset by Avon Dataset Ltd, Bidford-on-Avon, Warks
Printed and bound in Great Britain by
Mackays of Chatham PLC, Chatham, Kent

Hodder Children's Books
A division of Hodder Headline plc
338 Euston Road
London NW1 3BH

For Jane Gardam

One

DIARY 23rd June. My name is (~~Victora~~) Victoria
Wendy Hempstall. I am spelling like a baby, but
I can't do little ones writing any more, it's a
sort of drawing, and this is joined up. I am too
old for a child, nearly 14teen. Actuly I was still
12 at Earster, but definately born, which
hapens, I feel curled up like an embrio, of cause.

I have Robin and Fran, perants. Other people
have mummy and so on. They have gone out
today. They have gone away again when I was
having to go out riding. I know they have done
it before, because I cant (~~rember~~) remeber
about it, it wont come thruogh, its the same
fealing I cant bear it. My knees smell of horse.

This morning Fran did a joke making lunch. It
went (~~knocky knocy~~) gnocchi gnocchi (off the
HEMPSTALL HEMPSTALL HEMPSTALL pacquet) and so on,
whose there? pasta, pasta who? pasta parmer
zan, (HHH sprincling cheese). Robin went insain
because it made him luagh, it was a paneful
site, he thinks jokes (~~corupped~~) (crupt) damege
the intelagence and are wrong. He thinks his
mind is going.

Personaly I think so to. My knees are awful, they make my nose run, praps I am crying but not sobing. There is (~~sumthing~~) (~~sumething~~) somthing wrong.

Evrything is more than wrong. All so that boy is watching me. I think his name is Paw. I dont know if he said it that way. The (~~lillapu~~) Lilliputains call me Victorial. The boy is one of them and that is how they speak, Robin calls them Bolians, but it is nice boy. I shuold not of gone out this afternone, I am definately not crazy on riding.

That boy went by at Abots Lea with a traylor. Praps he thought it was my home. He does not know where I live. No body knows where I live. I wish some body knew. I wish I did.

Paul had not known where she lived. He plodded away at it, like a man finding a wild bees' nest. You follow a bee a little way, and lose sight of it. But stand still, and another comes by, and you follow that again. If night comes you mark the place you are in and go home. You return the next day and wait again and at last you are led to the nest.

But the girl was a solitary insect, and all the others, in that hat and that coat, were from other nests, and could not lead him there. He had had to identify before tracking, and could not often be at the start of the trail.

In other countries, never your own, helpful birds lead you to the comb and wait for reward, buying and selling wares not their own; but here and now neither were girls of any school.

It bothered Paul not to be able to recall exactly when he had noticed the first bee, when she had meant honey, or some element of come-hither. He had forgotten why he had gone to her school. The near reason was easy: he had gone that way to meet Angela, and there is nothing memorable about meeting a sister. He had carried something for Angela, or to her, but did not now know what the thing was, or which time, because it came to him gradually that there had been a time before which had become a ghost on his recordings. Not knowing the occasion, there was nothing he could associate with her, or the several things he might have carried or taken along for Angela. How could there have been no foreshadowing, no sign of the coming state?

The likeliest thing was the chrome music stand, which he and Angela needed on the same day. He wanted it during school, and she wanted it after school, and he could have been taking it to her. The possibility added a different quality to its bright metal, some autumnal reminiscence beyond the occasional reflected schoolroom or cloud; or that mocking glitter when he was conscious of a wrong note, some fault of embouchure, what Mr Glennister would reproach as the Bristol elephant, with more meaning than he would admit.

On one of those autumnal days, then, Angela was being prefect to a younger girl. Angela's head bobbed up and down a little as she laid down a school rule, and the younger girl was looking up with a very set face, lips folded in and hidden, eyes fixed to the brain only, behind guilty glasses, ears somewhere under hat and fair hair, listening to far-off things but hearing Angela, enduring. They were on the stone steps outside a door, against the sky, connected by the iron guard rail, and beyond them the trees still had a trimming of red leaves.

Paul thought it was then that Angela said, 'Such a silly girl. She forgets to go home.' But it might have been one wet day of winter, about the same younger girl, for Angela was often, indeed always, in the same prefectorial state of herself. Was the other girl the same one? She was for Paul: even if it was not so in fact it had become truth for him; they had identity: the pain of sorting it out was more than the pain of being wrong.

This time she was walking away across the wet asphalt of the yard on her own reflection (not itself completely identical), head looking down, legs moving to walk, but the rest keeping still and pretending not to be the person spoken to. O lucky asphalt able to hold the image of its mirroring, like the bitumen of Judaea. Paul was pleased and baffled by this image of his own devising, putting together observation and knowledge of early photography learnt at school.

'Did I see that one before?' he asked, watching original and echo, to the gate and out of being.

'Very likely,' said Angela.

'The one that doesn't go home?' said Paul.

'She does now,' said Angela. 'She used to go down with her friends to the Centre and get a bus there to places she didn't live in, and then walk miles back home. Perhaps she isn't a very satisfactory girl. You don't want to be interested.'

'I think she'd be all right,' said Paul.

'If you ask me, I'd say that was only a guess,' said Angela, prefectorializing him with a look. 'She's funny people.'

'It's always a guess,' said Paul. 'I've seen the movie. What's her name?'

'She says it's Wendy,' said Angela. 'But the class list has her initial V, so I don't really know. She has make-believe habits, Paul.'

Paul considered what Angela said. She was a very steady person, assumed that everyone ought to be the same, and surely wanted to be, and helped them in that direction.

'I think I might be getting some make-believe habits myself,' Paul said. He handed over the music stand, took a parcel, or did whatever had to be done at that time and went out of the gate into the road.

It was the end of the trail for him that day. The girl called approximately Wendy was out of sight round some corner, far off in the forest trails of Clifton streets.

It was not long before Christmas, close against the end of term. The few days remaining had not allowed him to follow the final bees to the nest. If he had been able to come the way past Angela's, and the girl's, school in time each day he might have managed it, but twice a week he was late out and could not be there.

'You're going a long way about it, Paul,' said Angela one morning as they walked over the Downs. 'Why not declare your interest? Approach. Offer to carry homework. I think that's what happens, though it never did to me.'

'Because if she didn't want to know,' said Paul, 'I wouldn't be able to go on looking at her because I'd know it was a nuisance. I still have to find out where she lives, and whether I can or not. I'd better do that first. There would be no point in doing it afterwards if it was hopeless. It's better to have hope, anyway.

Hope's part of a thing, and belongs to it.'

'I don't hope until I'm sure,' said Angela. 'Then I know what I'm hoping for.'

'I hope I like what I find,' said Paul. 'I don't know what it is. I have to find it first.'

'Hempstall,' said Angela. 'Her name, like those supermarkets, but I don't think it is.'

'No,' said Paul, shying away from this random definition. 'It'll be a cousin.'

Angela gave him one of her looks, because he had rejected what she said. However, prefectorial looks do not weigh quite so much at home. Paul said no more.

The term closed with getting him further than a tangle of streets somewhere beside the Suspension Bridge, and a bus stop in Pembroke Road. He marked the spot where he last saw her flying home, and waited until next term. He had wanted, though, to be able to show her what he was doing this winter at Nailsea, what all the family was doing these days, in a cold barn. He wanted to measure that activity against reality, her against the activity.

That activity, that project was well on its way. It was scheduled for completion and use by Midsomer Fayre. They went out to it on the afternoon of Christmas Eve.

The work of departure was already done. The little trailer was loaded and ready to hitch. Dad came home early from work and was into his overalls almost before the door closed behind him. Paul had spent some time the night before ticking off the list in the garage and making validation tests. That meant putting a pressure gauge on the gas cylinders, counting the tools, opening and dipping the oil-cans, sniffing to see that the pot called turpentine was turpentine, that paint was paint of the indicated and required colour, kind and quantity, that wood of the size and texture needed was ready to load, that cordage was there, that canvas was rolled and ready, that there were lamp bulbs and wire and that the batteries were charged and filled, that the two spare wheels were in place and full of air.

'Little tool-kit,' said Dad, round a tomato sandwich of late dinner. 'We do want that.'

'And our teas,' said Mum. 'Now Martin, you jump in Tina, and Dad and Paul and I will pull up the trailer and you can check the lights.'

Martin was Paul's younger brother. Tina was the car. The last car had been a Cortina of that name, and the present one still held the name though it was a 1964 Zephyr. Vintage, Dad said. Paul, maintaining the same view, suspected an ageing of style in the bodywork and the suspension, without losing faith in the classification.

'Yes, of course he's eccentric,' said Angela once, about Dad. 'Are you going to tell him?'

When they were hitched up, Martin tested the lights of the trailer, and they were ready to leave. Mum was in the front with Dad, and the rest of them in the back. Paul was behind the driver, Martin in the middle, and Angela had the littlest one on her knee, as well as the basin.

Paul was wondering whether it wasn't time to call his little sister by a better name than the one she had now, Tiny Wee. It seemed to him that he didn't want to say that any more. No one else seemed to worry about it, though. He thought she might be given a better name for Christmas, perhaps; if she was called by her true name she did not respond: she did not know she was Marion. Some extension of family eccentricity, he remembered, had called him Bomber until he went to school, and he was not sure why.

Now Marion was waiting to be sick, by any other name.

'Has it happened yet?' asked Mum, at the top of Blackboy Hill, communicating through the driving mirror.

'We think it'll be on the bridge again,' said Martin.

Nobody minded much, not even Tiny Wee, but it was better if it happened where they could stop and rinse the basin.

It was the bridge again. 'It's more like being airsick,' said Martin. 'High up like this and all the little houses down below.' The bridge was the Suspension Bridge slung over the gorge.

'The first thing they had here,' said Dad, 'was an iron bar six hundred feet long, stretched out over that drop, like a continuous rail. You might have got dizzy then.'

'One eight one, point eight one eight one eight metres,' said Angela, unnecessarily and within three seconds – having counted on her fingers. Paul saw.

'Six hundred,' said Dad. 'Whatevers.'

They had the stop for the basin, and to wipe Tiny Wee's face, and then went straight on to the barn at Nailsea.

''Tis cold, and the light going,' said Mum.

'We have to press on, Mum,' said Paul. 'Six months and we have to be on the road.'

'I don't need reminding that it's midwinter,' said Mum, looking around, satisfied with twilight and with the observing of it. 'Better out of the house some times.'

'We'll just set up now, and then go back,' said Dad, anxious not to have mutiny, wondering whether his own delight with what he was doing still extended to the rest of the family. 'We'll be an hour or two, that's all. This isn't a working day. Leave that until tomorrow, when it's all clear, no one about, no calls on time.'

She's not saying a word about no Christmas dinner, no lazing round the table while she sweats in the kitchen, thought Paul. She's steady, like Angela. She'll shiver with us out here. It's for him, it's for us; it's for the thing itself.

There was no more time for thinking what tomorrow was not to be. Even for Paul, his mind mostly on the small streets beside the bridge, and someone who lived somewhere there, there was no time for anything but what was being done here and now.

The first thing was to set up a heat-centre, a gas burner at the back of the barn. Even before that there was some moving to do of the things already in the building. The things in there were on trailers, propped and chocked, precious and valuable, each worth more for what you felt about it than for what you could get paid for it. Four trailers had to be hauled away from the back wall of the barn. Four sheets of asbestos roofing had to be set up to form a room, before the heater could be brought in and clicked into life. Then an old car seat was put beside it and Mum and Tiny Wee put down to play there.

Mum would rather have been out working with the rest of them, but Tiny Wee had to be occupied. If Mum thought, now the reality came to her again, that she could have stayed at home, warm, she did not say so. She joined in with the project as much as anyone else.

The trailer they had brought was backed up to the doors and brought in. A bench along the wall was laid with tools from it. A gas lamp was lit, and electric inspection lamps, run from the batteries in the trailer, were made ready.

Dad got out the plans. The irreplaceable hand-drawn copy of them was in the bank, so he had brought a photo-copy. It was set up above the bench, and they were ready.

'Third trailer,' said Dad. 'We're doing platform rods now. Let's get it out and ready, and we can be into it tomorrow first thing.'

Trailer three was manoeuvred to the front and stood there shapeless, lit by greyish afternoon light from one side, and by the gaudy but wan glare of the gas at the other. Paul lit up one of the inspection lamps and pulled aside a fold of the tarpaulin cover. He held the lamp and looked within. 'All right in here,' he said. 'Let's get it undone.'

They got it undone. Mum and Tiny Wee came to watch. The surprise and happiness never went away. Out of the formless canvas mounded on the trailer came four bright fairground horses, leaping into the sullen day with open nostrils and eager mouths, fresh under the canvas, seeking the open fields of day and night, moving in their stillness.

Once again all feelings about eccentricity went away. The horses could not be resisted, the ride they were part of, parked in pieces on the trailers, was their vivarium, and they had to be displayed actually moving and simulating life, giving rides round and round their platform.

10

'Ah,' said Dad, humble before a greater reality. 'I do wait to see they every time,' and Tiny Wee had to be lifted up to stroke the gay paint.

Perhaps we all reach further than the paint, the gilt, the dappled pigment, Paul thought, to ride a mile away.

'Enough of foolishness,' said Dad. 'Work to do. But my God, they do be beautiful.'

'Ride on horsey,' said Tiny Wee.

'Wait half a year,' said Dad. 'We'll have them proper this time, like 'twas before you were born, little maid.'

Two

DIARY 23rd June, a bit later. Actuly I do baby spelling all the time, it is a faze of not being able to spell exalently, because there isn't any provation whats wrong if it all is. Fran doesn't care, but Robin thinks that wrong spelling and jokes arent alowd and numbers are wrong too, that is true for me to. He goes insain if he hears a pugn. {(~~He says they are~~ (~~ambuos~~) (~~amgubus~~) (~~ambiug~~))}. My knees are getting wurse.

This house is like the Great Britan floteing in the sea without a person on it exept the brekafast cooking on the table, they have all gone out no body knows where they have not even washupped the lunch stuff or only a bit, the knives down in the cloth not dried, if there were saifty belts they wuold not of been thrown out. Its lunch here, the brekafast was on the ship. I wish they had'nt (~~thuogt~~) thougt of riding, I am definately only pretending to be crazy about it. it's not quiet like theyve gone out its quiet like theyve gone away, theyre wurse than not here. Its like a pugn on kinds of silance. I am curled on the rug like Granny Hempstall. I am her (~~embroidery~~) embrio again, now that Fran has given me up. ~~But Granny Hempstall has~~ I wondre why we had knives for lunch when it was only (~~knocky~~) (~~gnochi~~) gnocchi, Fran uses a fork and so do I but Robin has to use a baby spoon. I have been to the kitchen twice and looked at the spelling, also they are size 19 minuti I wonder what theyre like size 50 hugi. Its Fran of coarse size 50 and it hasnt worked again, it didnt last time thats how I know it must of hapened before. I shuoldnt ever in my life of gone in that room. It was my best room. Now it is disproved of.

I remeber I wore out my genes and my (~~ke~~) pance and my actul (~~bot~~) boddy. I did not keep a DIARY then, Id never heard of them. I dont think I cuold of writen much then I was too little when we found the room.

'Look, Vict, a secret passage,' Robin was calling from a long way off, somewhere beyond the beginning of Victoria's memory.

'She's just in bed,' said Fran. 'She didn't hear; we can leave it until tomorrow.'

But Victoria had heard in bed, and said so.

'A quick look only,' said Fran. 'Do you hear, a quick look only, both of you. It's been a long day.'

'All days should be long,' said Victoria, feeling this one illimitably behind her, starting with the first atom of history.

'Vict,' said Robin again. He seemed to be somewhere along

his secret passage and not hearing either of them.

'Coming,' said Victoria, slowly, going into bed and getting out at the same time. There was a warm piece of mattress that she let her side stay on long enough for her toes to find a hot water bottle wrapped in a towel. The toes stayed on it just for a moment, to feel the warm, and then for another moment, to make sure of it. Then she knew it was not a hot water bottle in a towel but a large black cat coiling round her feet.

After that it was morning. Someone was dinging the pipes of the radiators. The black cat had turned colourlessly into a flabby bottle of lukewarm, and a towel that was a roughness in the bed, an empty cat.

Someone was mending the hot water system. It wasn't Robin, because he couldn't do machines at all, not even his computers. Fran had to drive the car if it was a long journey; and he never put lids on liquidizers.

It had been a long way yesterday. It had been about as long as going on a holiday, and much further than going to the farm. Yesterday morning Victoria had thought they would come to the same rooms again, because they were moving house. Everybody said they were moving house. But you move everything except the house. You get all your belongings, but they are in a muddle, and you get a lot of newspaper.

Victoria had not known about diaries, but she had the invention ready in her mind. She went through yesterday in order:

the furniture going into a huge van;

the breakfast things being washed but not dried because a man she had not seen before had packed up the cloth;

everything going out when it was already safe in the house, but thinking she would not ask about it;

in the car and waiting while Fran had a last look and Mrs budgie from one of the other houses gave her a kiss and a packet of gums;

Mr smokapipe from the house on top telling Robin he would like it in Bristol;

off in the rain;

taking keys to the office, not Robin's office at the College;

lunch on the way a great dish of stuff all wooden and huge, more than Robin could eat, and he knew about groceries but pretended not to;

Robin paying with a many-pound note and getting real money back;

wanting to go shopping with it in the shop and people getting cross, well, Robin and Fran;

a lovely fine afternoon at Bristol;

a lovely fine evening by the time Fran had found the way to an office there, and they got the key again;

Victoria knowing there must be a reason why they had not brought it with them;

finding the furniture in a new house, or just coming in as they got there;

a man saying it was a bloody steeplechase up they stairs;

at the end of carrying furniture he said 'Cheers,' to Robin when he got another of Robin's big pound notes;

drive straight back, he said, another load tomorrow;

but we've got everything, thought Victoria;

a lot more newspaper in the new house, or new flat;

rusty water coming out of the taps, all cold;

the house all cold as well;

nothing outside the windows except sky, and in one place a treetop, down below;

seeing birds fly from on top, but it might have been aeroplanes;

being here, the same person born into a different world.

They had gone out for tea and to get warm again. Then they had wasted all the warmness by going for a walk along a narrow road with chains overhead and sky each side. Robin had his camera. Victoria could see further by looking through it, seeing the photograph that was going to be there when you pressed it, stiff and flat. Before you press the button it is a moving picture. Just afterwards it does something interesting, Fran says. Then it is fuzzy again looked at without the camera.

Through the camera, safe on its strap, they were on a high bridge. There was a bumpy road far below. When Victoria talked about it Fran explained that she was seeing the river, and that the tiny path down there beside it was the road. 'That's not a bus but a steamer,' she said, taking the camera from Victoria. 'In case you fall off,' she said.

Two miles down, Victoria thought. Now I know. She thinks the camera gets dizzy, that's all.

'Well, some measurable distance,' said Robin.

'It depends how far it is,' said Fran. That was perfect sense to Victoria; Robin knew there was nothing to say, and said it.

The water looks soft, Victoria decided.

As well as that river shining there was a town further along,

17

with houses climbing along the cliffs either side, the tops of which the bridge came from and went to.

'Which is ours?' Victoria asked. Her eyes watered with looking, or cold. Fran decided Victoria was tired.

'I don't know, Vict,' said Robin. 'It's one of them, because we can see the bridge from it, so someone standing on the bridge can see some of the house. I don't know the way yet.'

He never knew the way anywhere, Victoria thought. But he must of meant to come here, she said, somehow.

'Must have,' said Fran, agreeing and disagreeing, but not bothering to explain.

Victoria looked at Robin through the camera while Fran held it. Fran's coat smelt of car and cold air and Fran. Robin went fuzzy because he was too close, and even cameras are not perfect. She turned the lens and he came sharp again, his hair standing out from his head in bread-crust-coloured curls, and his moustache the same. And Fran's hair was long and fair and on her shoulders. Victoria's was fair and fine and just cut round at neck level. By Fran, not by a proper girl with smelly bottles and professional scissors and those lights that shine warm, and old ladies with poached eyes. Fran's eyes were huge in the lens, an end of bridge in each one.

They had walked back home from the draughty bridge. Victoria had helped Robin measure the cupboards while Fran made some beds. Fran had boiled a kettle, poured a bottle, given Victoria a wash and put her into bed.

Now it was morning. Victoria was ready to recall what came next when the door opened and a man came in. 'Good mornen my dyurr,' he said. 'How bist thee, then?'

Victoria wondered who he was talking to, and what he was talking about, as well as what he was saying.

'What be your name?' he asked, not at all interested.

Victoria said her name.

'Victorial,' said the man, putting an 'l' on the end of it. 'That be a proper name year-bouts.'

He had a good strong smell, somewhere like burning forests. He leaned over her bed, tapped the radiator, then turned a key in the end of it, and it breathed. It spat and dribbled, gurgled and breathed again, spat and dribbled once more, and that was it. A moment later warmth came from it, alive and friendly.

'Right away there then, thic one be on line,' said the man; and he went out.

Victoria rolled over against the radiator. Then, when she was ready, she let herself remember about the secret passage. First she sorted it from dream into reality. It was real.

She knew it wasn't like Robin to talk about things being secret. For him a thing was there or not there, and it was only secret if you didn't know about it. Whether you knew about it, or didn't know, didn't alter what it was, so there was no need to say 'secret'. He must have thought it particularly good, to forget his rules.

She got up and went to see about things. There was nothing to think until she knew. She had worked through all yesterday's memory, and today was beginning before she had started it. She had an alarmed but satisfying thought that Robin and Fran might have taken the secret passage home and left her here with the strong-smelling man. Perhaps that was how life was done: she had moved and they had gone back and forgotten her the address.

The strong-smelling man had gone, leaving a tang of himself. Robin and Fran were preparing for breakfast. They were drinking coffee.

'What did that man smell?' Victoria asked. She was glad to see them. She did not want to stay with a man who did not know her name.

'Plumber,' said Fran. 'Resin, blowlamps, flux, oil, melted lead. Beer. Plumbers' wipes.'

'What are those?' asked Robin.

'Those swollen joints in lead pipes have to be wiped into shape,' said Fran. 'They use a special cloth.'

'I understand,' said Robin, like a machine. It was the same as a computer flashing a light at you, or beeping. Robin said that 'thank you' was not transactional: it had no place in sense, so he tried not to say it. He said 'I understand' instead. Fran said 'I do not understand' if she meant 'No thank you', and that made Robin cross, which computers can't be. It didn't stop him.

'What secret passage?' Victoria said next, wondering why a new house had an old packet of cereal and the same chipped butter dish with the old crumbed butter.

'We thought you hadn't heard that,' said Fran.

'Just before the cat sat on my feet,' said Victoria.

'Cat?' said Robin. 'What cat?'

'It was a hallu-singation,' said Victoria. 'As I fell asleep. I often get it. I quite like it. It's a different reallyality.'

'I think it's terrible,' said Fran, 'to teach the child how to look in her mind like that at seven years of age.'

20

'What secret passage?' said Victoria again. 'Or is my question being processed?'

'I had forgotten it,' said Robin, honestly but tiresomely.

'I understand,' said Victoria, loudly, angry lights flashing and bulbs bursting all over the circuit, like a fairground ride once, the cornflakes now tasting of sick, reminding her. Or perhaps the fairground ride was still in the future, and the thought was poured in later. Cornflakes taste of sick always. 'Perhaps it was hallu-singation again.'

'No, it's veridical,' said Robin. 'I mean, "It's veridical", the negative is not necessary.'

Neither Fran nor Victoria knew what the word meant. It turned out to mean that the secret passage was there. They went to see it at once.

It was in the hall of the flat. The way to it looked like an ordinary cupboard, with a door, the carpet stopping under it and dusty boards inside with round marks where paint has stood, and three different coat-hooks on one wall.

'First clue,' said Robin. 'Skirting board on two sides, right and left. They don't put that in cupboards.'

'You don't know that sort of stuff,' said Fran.

'I didn't tell him,' said Victoria. 'What's the use?'

'Second clue,' said Robin, hearing none of that, 'is outside the front door. It should have been the first clue.'

Victoria had to have it pointed out to her. They had thought that the flat was as high as the house went. But going on beyond it, its underslope showing over their heads, was another flight of stairs.

'Third clue,' said Robin. 'I took down the panel at the back of the cupboard, and saw what must logically be there.'

He took the panel down again. There were the missing stairs, going up and turning a corner.

'What's up there?' said Victoria.

'I haven't looked, Vict,' said Robin. 'It isn't part of the flat, so it's nothing to do with us. But it can't belong to anyone else.'

'We can go and look,' said Victoria. 'If we can't go and look why did you take the wall down?'

'I think I had a malfunction,' said Robin. 'System error.'

'You'll have to have a piece of Fran's chocolate at bedtime,' said Victoria. 'That's good for your system. I think only a silly person wouldn't go up straight away.'

'I think that's true,' said Robin. 'That is the proper program. When I read fiction, as a child, that was always done to secret passages.'

'Very dicule,' said Victoria.

They went up a step at a time. The steps were all good. There was nothing broken or rotten or difficult. They led to a room above Victoria's room. It had wallpaper with flowers and a shiny stripe. It had a window.

'It's like extra memory,' said Robin. 'Random access.'

'I can see the bridge,' said Fran, thinking about curtains.

Victoria looked. Without the camera it was nearly all sky, but there was a little tree waving not far away, and a blob that might be a bird. 'I'll wait for a photograph,' she said.

Fran came up and had a look. 'Leave this to me,' she said. 'We'll have to ask the agent about it, and I can see that you would get it all wrong. You'd say there was a room here, and can we use it, wouldn't you?'

'Exactly,' said Robin. 'Is there anything else to say?'

'Yes,' said Fran. 'Getting it the right way round. I'll ask him to tell me what would be the position if, and so on, there was a room. You can ask a computer that, can't you? "What if" is logical isn't it?'

'Yes,' said Robin. 'But . . .'

'If you say "but" you're only saying you know more about the question than you're asking; but that doesn't alter the question, does it?'

'You go and see the agent,' said Robin, switching off the conversation and closing down. 'The coffee will be getting cold.'

The agent came round later. 'It didn't work so well,' said Fran. 'They aren't logical down there.'

'We've got to be,' said the agent. 'I understand the panel came off in your hand, squire.'

'I lifted it down,' said Robin.

'That's hands,' said the agent. 'In human terms. Position is, Fire Regs. Can't let that room in with the flat, part and parcel, no way out of it by fire escape. But look, I prop this panel back where it was, I done my duty, no, no, you can't on no account use that room, so what you do is your own affair, you're just lucky. No, I won't have a cup of tea, can't hang around, sorry you got the inconvenience of another room, some people get all the trouble, tara.'

Some time later the room got a rug. And towards Christmas there was a muddle in Victoria's mind about a horse-box. She didn't know what it would be, and in the end it was an ordinary white Transit van, belonging to the farm and driven by Wendy. Wendy was then a sort of extra grandmother, which some people have a young one of. Wendy had brought two farm lads, and the horse itself was in a box inside the van. Fran had made explanations with no sense, but the truth was that the horse was in a box and the box was in the van, so the van was not the box. Or even the horse.

Victoria was delighted with the horse part of it because it was Robin's rocking horse from when he was a boy and lived at the farm, when Granny was still there and not Wendy. Victoria had never had any picture in her mind of a live horse, because she had thought all the time of a little box. What came was better than live, a rubbed brown leather with a black loving eye.

It was a pity it only got Robin when he was young, she thought. A pity, much more, that Robin only got Robin.

Wendy and the boys got it up all the stairs and into the secret room. It was like a day at the farm, with the boys talking in the farm Welsh way, and saying it was a luffly litt-el flut, Missez Emstul, indeed, and inviting Victoria to go back with them, nobody to look after us whatefer, they said, we all deserve a pretty lady I'm sure and they seem to run in the family, izzenet?

Victoria stayed with the horse. Almost at once she rode it so far and so fiercely that there was a message from the flat below about the rumbling, and she wore through her trousers at the bone, and got a blister in a place invisible to her, and, she hoped, to the rest of the world.

Three

DIARY 23rd June, a long time since lunch. Ive been in this bit before and I still dont know the (w-y) way. They must of told me too long ago. I dont know any one exept Mr Pattypatty downstairs and he dosnt know exept pattypatty on the head like a dog. Im writeing it down so it tells me, and it still dosnt have actul meaning. My hart is going (cnochi) gnocchi gnocchi, made of pasta, the sause sticking in my throat. Im sitting among the wrocks of my intalect, my intelagence only goes to the walls, it wont be sky out of the window and it isnt house through the door but fuszy lights. I should start at the beggining, because I dont know what hapened before then.

if i am not me who am i. they always wanted some body else i can tell.

THEY GOT ME. The way they arent here now is part of the beggining I remeber wrong. I remeber when they put up a blackbord at school the day after I got my glasses but it was there all the time. It was confuscing because of being used to fuszy, and then too clear, all tiny (brics and ston) bricks and stones but you do not look at them all seperet, the way you look is just like you hadnt glasses on. Exept you can see if you want, houses get strait egdes, and trees get bigger. If it is fuszy under the bridge one day it is clowds. Somtimes I do not want to see exscept just around me, like in a room. It is more holey to take them off in church, Saint Peter and Saint Paul. That time the boy was there and Fran said that stuff, she couldnt of appreuved but she isnt Robin so why was she funny. Robin does not go. Fran said he would if it was Saint Peter, Paul, and Wendy. Robin is roten soft on Wendy. I tried to telaphone her when I got to her name, but it was a Welsh boy so I put the reservoir down.

'The ironwork at St Matts,' said Dad. 'I do *like* that, pure Victorian, marvellous, like a old road engine, windows round as flywheels, aisles like a water-jacket, old organ whistling on corners, amen and such, driver in th'old pulpit twirling out a sermon to keep us on the road.'

'More like a railway station,' said Mum. She went to Holy Trinity most weeks; Dad, on occasional visits, chose different churches for different times. Now he was getting steam up and felt like St Matthew's, so Mum was happy to go with him, and Angela to go with her. Paul went up to his room again and put an envelope in his pocket. Martin's bed was empty and rumpled. Martin was in the next room with Tiny Wee.

'What are you doing?' Paul asked, because of the noise.

'We're into the chocolates,' said Martin.

'Be good, then,' called Mum from below. It was not necessary, because Martin was an acutely sensible boy, a sort of male Angela.

Paul felt the envelope to see that it was flat. The thing he was into this morning was useless, hopeless, but there was a possibility. It would be a comfort to have nothing but sense, like Angela, or nothing but a fulfilled passion, like Dad and his barn of gilded gallopers at Nailsea.

'I won't go with you,' Paul said, when he got downstairs. 'I'll go across the downs and see St Peter's.' He was sure he had seen Wendy, Victoria, Hempstall going into the building one morning at mattins time.

'Then we'll take Tina and drop you off the far side and save you a walk,' said Dad. His thoughtfulness in small things was unofficious, not militant like Angela's.

Angela looked at him, then stopped her mind intruding. 'Prayer book,' she said, getting her own.

Tina was outside, of course, the garage always too full for a car. After coming back last night in the rain Dad had gone out and washed Tina down, unofficious but relentless towards himself and his own standards. Paul was sure no one else in Bristol had done that, nor would he do it himself, though he would not have chosen not to, only been without the compulsion needed. I am foolishly without principle or wisdom, he thought. I am not even going to church for any of its reasons. Angela knows. God knows. I know. We are all sinners.

Tina took him to the end of Pembroke Road, and then turned away towards the ironwork of St Matthew's church. Paul was only a little way from St Peter and St Paul. He was early for the eight o'clock service. He half wondered about not going to it at all, about staying in the car and going with the others. I wish they did not understand, he thought. I wish they did. Why doesn't the world help?

But he had been brought here for that purpose, and Mum and Dad, and Angela, helpfully concerned with bringing him here and wanting him here, would expect him to go to the service. He knew it was so. His alternative now, of not going in at all, was rubbish: there was no point in walking round unknown streets looking for evidence of the unknown address of an almost unknown girl, at about eight o'clock on the morning of Christmas Day. Yet to wander was a temptation.

Being here at all was reasonable, because the hilly streets high with white stone houses, meant more to him than he could express, more than he knew how to feel. This was his only chance to be here on this day, and here he was. The card in its envelope lay in his pocket. It could be torn up later.

The last bell began to ring, and he followed it to the building, the last bee buzzing among organ pipes within?

There was polished pine, and something aromatic in the air – yesterday's pine logs hither? Paul felt uncomfortable and stupid, following his own footsteps and not being warmed at all.

The service began, different from the one he knew. He thought of the door, which had been closed behind him, and wondered whether he had made a strong mistake about the kind of church he had come to, and suspected the resiny smell was incense, the words hastily compiled from Latin, the whole thing to do with Rome. But no one at home had said anything.

28

Possibly it was one of those occasions the experience of which would cure him of trying again. There were many of those in life. It was a sign, perhaps, that he had come over here against the general meaning of his career, and was here foi folly. Or his presence was a compulsion, like washing Tina in the rain. He dropped a hymn book, picked it up, and was part of this gathering, soothing its rumpled leaves.

Now he had to sit, or stand or kneel, where he was, keeping time with the rest of the congregation. He found, as he went on, that the words were the same but in a different order: not a question of the Lord's Prayer backwards, but of having it where it was not expected.

He thought he might be being superstitious, looking for signs about luck in places where there were no signs; where there could be no signs. How could he be getting a special message among all these other people, when there was hardly any information being passed through; a few words among them all? He would have got just as little, or as much, by walking round the streets.

All at once he got the sign. It was more than a sign; it was the thing itself, what he had come for.

She was there. She was sitting, or in a pew, about eight ahead of him, on the other side. It seemed to him that his head came into being round him, and that he had just woken up for that day. In fact he had been awake some time with Martin and his stocking, and then Tiny Wee and hers, and then both of them together in one room or another, and then some complicity with Dad about certain parcels to go in Tina's boot for later in the day. So he had been awake, but not collected together.

29

The rest of the service became a jumble to him. He tried to find his way through in order, because he reckoned all the parts would be there. But it was no good, he made nothing out of it. He stayed kneeling when the rest went to communion. He said, look, I'm here, but I don't know my way round, and if you did it on purpose, thank you. No one replied. It was curiously unfulfilling, as if he were still somewhere else, only his shell kneeling or standing, functional but useless.

And the message, the giving, was not a gift of God, only of luck; or maybe from watching the bees fly in and out from their nest, in honeyed domesticity.

He saw her full face, and nakedly without her glasses. It seemed proper, and improper. This time her eyes were not fixed on Angela's, or cast down to the ground. They were not like her walking-home eyes. They had always seemed to get her home, but unglazed they were not much help to her in church. She had left them under some sweet pillow. His mind stopped, uneasy in a strange house, or filled with Martin and Tiny Wee on pillows horrible with chocolate.

She came back from the altar rails to her place alone, with her mother (Paul thought) somewhere behind her. She did not know which row she had been sitting in, and was peering into each one. Her mother came up behind and set her right. If she hadn't, Paul dreamed, she might have come up close to him, asked the way, smiled, needed help.

He slid the card out of his pocket and laid it on the hymn-book shelf. How strange that such a thing should be ready, as well as its occasion. There must at some time have been valid, if vain, functions in his mind, but most preparation is of little

30

account; there is no way of checking the tool kit or the batteries of the unknown, validating the power and the paint of the unforeseeable.

The service ended for the rest of the congregation. For Paul it had not begun, and he would have liked an instant replay, but that was not in prayer books old or new.

He stood up. The girl came along the aisle, nearing him. He would follow her out, catch up in the porch, and present the card. It was the card they had all used this year, with the gallopers on it, and season's greeting inside. The girl came past. Paul wanted to jump out and give her a hundred cards.

She did not see him. Why should she? She walked with her mother. In a brown skirt, stockings with a small white hole beside one ankle, brown leather shoes with a frilled flap on the instep, a green sweater, and a bronze coat. She was quite plain, but unearthly beautiful; there was nothing else like her, and her uniqueness was the reason for all creation.

Except me, Paul thought. I am the one who has seen her. To them she's just their Angela, or Wendy, or Victoria; but to me . . .

Something scuttered along the carpet by his feet. It was a pair of glasses, doing a little bounce before lying down and staring at the ground. Paul picked them up and looked about to see who had dropped them. Plenty of people were passing. He stood there holding them while the congregation moved along. Now it was all going wrong. The girl was nearly out of sight, and Paul was waiting for some person to come back and look on the ground, delayed, thwarted, acceding to some unexplained code of polite behaviour, hiding behind it and being too cowardly to take a positive step himself.

31

For some reason he could not imagine, the girl and her mother came back down the aisle, and to their place in the pews. 'You should keep them on,' the mother said, scolding in a muted in-church fashion. 'Then you'd have some chance of finding them when you'd put them down.'

Paul felt a fool in the face of this humble logic: they had come back for the glasses and card he was holding. He stepped forward with them and held them out. The mother took them, and said 'Oh, thank you,' handing back the card, as if it had been a mistake. Paul had to make a great effort of will to do the next thing, which was giving the girl the card into her hand, pushing it forward with his own uncompliant one. It was equivalent to the effort Dad expended in going out and washing Tina after a busy, dirty day. Or it was more than that. Dad would end with a clean car, and Paul expected to be reproached and reproved.

Now the girl was getting two things thrust at her at the same time; the glasses were going to her in the way things do that mothers are giving you, very here-and-now; the card was wavering about, Paul felt, and not being very convincingly proffered. Or at least not very elegantly.

'It isn't ours,' said the mother, but by then the girl had ignored the glasses and taken the card. She was getting it open, too. It was just the way Tiny Wee got things open, like a little girl, a child. What if she were only nine years old? How can I tell? I only know Angela, who is adult, and Tiny Wee, who is a nickname. Angela said she must be, well, thirteen by now, a silly age. Unless you were Angela, who had never been a silly age.

The mother went on to say, 'You two must know each other, then.' It seemed as if she expected them to be able to know each other. 'Vict, you've never told me your friend's name.'

'What friend?' said the girl. 'I don't know his name.'

'He knows yours,' said the mother.

'I don't,' said Paul.

'It's your face, not your fortune, obviously,' said the mother. 'I'm Fran Hempstall. Now you both tell me your names and I'll introduce you to each other.'

She must know her daughter's name, thought Paul. But it was not so queer as he supposed at first, when he remembered that the girl used two names, one in her mouth, another on the class list. The girl considered for a little while.

'My name is Victoria Hempstall,' she said.

'My name is Paul Creasey,' said Paul.

'Victoria,' said Fran, 'this is Paul Creasey; Paul this is Victoria Hempstall.'

'How do you do, Paul,' said the girl. 'Is that right?'

'How do you do, Victoria,' said Paul. His own words echoed chatteringly from the vaults and arches of the building, and were absorbed by carpety kneelers.

Meanwhile Fran looked at the card, front and back. She moved on out of the church as well. Paul was very cold, all at once. He wanted to be able to say something about the picture on the card, the galloping horses, but there was nothing to say. If he knew about them, then so did all the rest of the world, and it would be tiresome to say it. They got to the street outside without words, all three together.

'Happy Christmas,' said the girl. 'We're just having software for dinner. Logical boneless turkey.'

'Merry Christmas,' said Paul, uncertain what to make of the

statement. 'We're having sandwiches for ours.'

He turned away and walked towards the Downs. He was working out that he might have time for a quick look back by going across one of the little parallel roads, to see which way Victoria went. But Tina drew her low bulk next to him, and he got in beside Angela. He smelt the soft communion wine on her breath.

Then it was breakfast. After it, Mum took him aside and showed him a number of parcels and bundles and baskets, and asked him to stow them secretly in the car to take with them to Nailsea. She was not going to be done out of giving presents and making a dinner, wherever they were to spend Christmas.

Four

DIARY is the nearest thing to me, exactly the
same date but an inch later in afternoon time.
Im not aloud to tell lies anywhere else, Robin
says theyre ilogical, but ilogical is there even if
it dosnt do what you (~~whant~~) want. But
sometimes it does. If sombody makes a mistake
either that is not a lie. I WILL TELL LIES IN MY
DIARY I will work out how my intelagence goes
as far as I can see, but first I will remeber how
the boy Paw calls me Victorial. Robin says he is
a Lilliputain. I thought he was going to fly, ever
so long ago. Why do I remeber one bit about
him, Robin is all ways like that?

Long ago another walk on the bridge, and Robin quarrelling
with the air. The air was quarrelling with the bridge, making it
move underfoot even when there was no traffic on it. Fran was
sailing through all these blowings, and Victoria was riding a fish
between them, before them, and after them, in the river below
at a right angle to the bridge.

'They're tying me down,' Robin was saying. 'I'm not getting
anything done. I've got something to find out, research; I've
had it agreed and now it isn't happening. This is important, too

35

important for commercial interests to take over. It is pure research.'

'Perhaps you could hear their side of it,' said Fran. 'They must have something to say.'

'No,' said Robin, 'they haven't got a side. They're all fiddly fiddly fiddly about different things, fiddly fiddly fiddly about their rights and positions. "I've done all I can," they say, but they mean they've done all they will. And they're tying me down. They're giving in to outside interests, vested interests, playing politics with my department.'

'You can't see that they have to be like that,' said Fran. 'They've got to work to live, they live for tomorrow, and there isn't really very much work, so they sit there and polish the edges.'

'Stop talking in metaphors,' said Robin. 'Talking in metaphors lets you tell lies and become illogical.'

'Me?' said Fran.

'People,' said Robin. 'Not you; people.'

'You don't have to work,' said Fran. 'Not for the University anyway. Your father could probably buy you a department of your own, if you wanted.'

'No,' said Robin. 'That's commercial too. I'm going to find my own way. There's no one more commercial than my father, though at least it isn't a vested interest; a grocer doesn't need encryption systems, for one thing. It's not logical to live on his money, and I never have. I shall never have any of it and I don't want it. No, I've got to work like anyone else, because that's a logical principle. But they're tying me down. I'm like Gulliver being tied down by the Lilliputians.'

'How's about a metaphor, then?' said Fran.

'Lilliput,' said Robin, leaning on the rail of the bridge and looking upstream. 'All the little houses full of midgets.'

'Metaphor, metaphor, metaphor,' said Fran to Victoria.

'Gallop, gallop, gallop,' said Victoria, on a fast fish.

'Sometimes I think I could walk over them all,' said Robin, stamping his feet.

'You'll have the bridge broken,' said Fran. 'Let's get on into the woods, and you can walk a few trees down.'

'Yes, come on,' said Robin. 'Being cross isn't sense, because facts are facts, no matter what I think of them.'

In the woods, he made Fran become cross in a sensible way by walking in all the mud he could find, and then managed to prove it wasn't there.

All the same, he had another muttering about things on the way back across the bridge. 'Bolians,' he called them this time, saying that he had invented a new category and that was the name of the people in it, so it wasn't metaphor or a simile, just a name.

Fran thought the word might be a bit rude, but never explained anything interesting to Victoria.

Five

DIARY 23rd June this year still. I think I can all so tell truth in my DIARY, and that is about the blackbord. That was more complacated than I said. I thougt it was there when I could see it, becaus I had seen it before. I thougt (~~it~~) the blackbord was not there when I was too far off to see it, and it was the same for evrything, but most of all becaus they kept talking about it even when I could not see it. But it was strange to look up and see it (~~existing~~) (~~ex~~) that word cannot be right it probably does not (exist). I wondre if that is logic. I am somtimes a bit (~~thic~~) (~~thique~~).

I am curtain they are not here, but it is difarent way of not being here, it feels very all gone. I am trying to stand up. Actuly I am writing this from on the loo and I am wondreing about a problem of pressing the button because it is so quiet here I do not want to make faital noise. I will stay sitting here while I press it.

I remeber when I was little I sank down in and Fran pressed the button she did not know I

had my pance on. It was like the island. I
wonder if they will come in during the noise. I
got splashed. I got splashed on the island, and I
got drunc. Praps I had better start remebering
them. On the way I will change my genes
becaus my actul bare knees are ok. And what I
am on my way to is finishing drying the knives
becaus the yellow cloth is from the island. I
have to wait until the loo stops filling and it
gets back to silance in the flat, even Mr Pattypatty
not doing a thing. Silance is bursting in loudly.
We took Grandpa's present to the island.

The present was the holiday itself on the island of Myros.

It had been early morning in Athens, and not warm, with
rain shaking down. The man who met them had very strange
teeth, with gold stripes, Victoria remembered. Perhaps that was
why he had never learned to speak, and it was hardly possible
to understand him. Fran had a little book. Victoria thought it
must be instructions on how to bring up men in other countries
so that they were sensible. The man with the striped teeth
could talk to other men there easily. He went out into the
street and stopped a car by putting his hand out and catching it.
Men shouted at each other in a cheerful cross way, waving hands.

They all got into the car, and went away down the long city.
Not even the words on shops could be read, or only a letter
here and there. There are dreams like that. 'Did I pack my
brain?' Victoria asked. She had to explain to Fran what she
meant.

'It's a different language and different letters,' said Fran.

'Can we still use ours?' said Victoria.

'Yes,' said Fran.

'Good,' said Victoria. 'I want to go to the toilet.'

But she had to wait until they got to the ferry. They were all day aboard that boat. The toilets smelt, but it was only the paint. Then they were at some houses by the sea, with no one about except old ladies in black and some boys in red trousers.

They walked along the rocks at the edge of the sea, and when the ferry went away the sea splashed up on Victoria's legs like cool boiling water and tightened her clothes on her.

They went up to the monastery the afternoon after next. Fran said she had had enough for the time being of lying in the sun, and she was sure some crabs had marked her down for a meal, and she wanted to disappoint them. Victoria had stayed in the villa the day before, because she had become a little sore with the sunshine, and something had given her a wobbly tummy. Fran said it couldn't be the food, since she ate hardly any of it. Still, she was cured of the wobbliness, and of not being able to touch the food, by the end of the monastery day.

Victoria had discovered a group of donkeys and wanted to stand by them at all times while they were fed on hard-looking leaves and prickly plants. In the end Robin had to pick her up. She struggled but the donkeys were not yet faithful and did not help. They looked at their grey salad and turned it over peevishly with their pouted lips.

'My legs are working; yours aren't,' said Robin.

Victoria could not see why she had to go to the monastery. 'You could run a program with me staying here and you going,' she said. 'Is that sense?'

41

'It's a non-viable alternative,' said Robin.

Victoria got ready for her last logical protest, a great big yell into Robin's ear. She had to look back to get at the ear, and when she saw the donkeys again, and coming towards her, she clicked her fingers at them. Robin thought that was very unchildish, but she had caught it from Grandpa and this was his holiday, so he should be represented.

Robin began to stride away. She clicked her fingers again and the donkeys began to follow.

'What's the matter?' said Robin. 'You aren't yelling.'

'The donks are coming,' said Victoria. 'I called them.'

She knew she had not called them. Two boys were driving them along by hitting their back legs with a stick.

'Stop it at once,' said Robin. 'I'll give you a ride right up the hill.'

'I'll choose my one,' said Victoria.

'No,' said Robin. 'I mean that you can ride on my back. I don't mean anything about donkeys, not now; perhaps after. They're not part of the program now. A sub-routine later.'

But the donkeys were now. They were the ride up to the monastery. Robin had not thought of going up the hill on a donkey: he had thought of walking to the monastery and a ride along a beach where it was flat, and only children were allowed; and he had known it would be impossible to arrange without knowing the right Greek words and syntax. The Greek letters meant mathematical things to him, but not to these Greeks. They didn't even mean sensible English words.

Before much could happen in the way of yelling by Victoria, she, Robin, Fran, and the donkeys and two boys had arrived in

42

a little square of the town, where other people were waiting, handbaggy ladies dressed in apricot linen and indoor trousers, and their men with outdoor faces on. All the people and animals together turned into a crowd. Victoria got down and took a donkey. Before Robin could say anything about not having a ride, a boy had taken Victoria and put her on the donkey, on a wooden saddle. She sat there behind the ears and had her feet smelled by the donkey's head, turned back and upside-down.

'Afro-thetay,' said the boy.

'Aphrodite,' said Fran. She was having to get on to a donkey too, and so was Robin. He did not see that it was possible to ride anywhere on something smaller than himself. He could have carried the donkey. And his legs were too long to stay off the ground.

Then they were going. Not very well, because the donkeys were not interested in the matter. It was a question of raising enough dust, Victoria thought. The dust all came from the donkeys, because they would not go if the boy pulled them, they would not go for 'Gee up', or for the silly things that people shrieked, like 'Mush', 'Ride 'em cowboy', and 'Geronimo'. They went only when the boys, of which there were now many more than two, whacked them with sticks. The donkeys lifted their tiny feet in the dusty sunshine and walked on bare rock up the hill, taking no notice.

'I say, keep away from the edge,' said Robin. They were going up a narrow way up the hill, and there was a rocky cliff to one side. Fran said it was a precipice. 'Look the other way,' she said.

'If anything happens to your donkey, Victoria, jump off the other side,' said Robin.

First I've got to get to Australia, thought Victoria. That's the other side. What could happen to a donkey? It is a perfect animal. Aphrodite had a string of blue beads round her ears. Her coat was like a dog's.

'Good luck,' said the boy, touching the beads and explaining them. But he had to beat the donkey to make it go. Victoria wondered whether he had to beat her as well, which he was doing, for it didn't make her go any faster.

The monastery was hot, high, smelly, dark, broken, old and covered with golden holy drawings inside. The men had long hair in buns, and beards, and black dresses. Victoria went round with everyone, lit a candle with them all, and looked forward to the ride down again.

So they had the ride down again. Robin found it as uncomfortable as illness. He sat upright and could not breathe. Victoria leaned forward. Fran walked all the way down and scraped her toes as she came.

'God,' said Robin, when they had got off the donkeys in the square again, and he and Fran and Victoria were together again after Victoria's visit to the loo. 'I need a drink. I thought the donkey had the worst of that kind of work, but I don't think so now. I had the worst of it.'

'And it didn't even kick you,' said Fran. 'One of the other people got kicked.'

'Mine was a more subtle donkey,' said Robin. 'Let's have a drink.'

Victoria drank her lemonade all at once. She drank Robin's

milky-looking drink in another go. When she had swallowed it she found it had been totally revolting and nasty, and the taste was pulling her tongue off. While she was beginning to tell them about the sheer horror of having drinks like that on the table, or in the world, something happened inside, and the drink, Robin's as well as her own, jumped out of her mouth on to the stones of the square. There were one or two bits of bread as well.

'Now she's being sick,' said Robin. He hated that.

'No, I'm not,' said Victoria. 'It was just a very nasty drink I got drunk on. I didn't want to keep it. I'll have to have some more lemonade. Also, I am very hungry now and I could eat anything.'

'A horse?' said Fran, while a boy sluiced water round their feet and scolded Victoria, and Victoria grinned.

'Not a donk,' she said. 'Never.'

She began to like any other food. She ate a Greek shepherd's pie without shepherd on top, and a lovely soapy pudding, but could not close her mouth on a white cardboardy vegetable tasting like empty boxes of Edinburgh rock.

Four times more she went to the monastery with the donkeys, walking all the way up each time, and riding down once when a donkey was empty of rider. She learnt to whip them along, and she learnt several Greek shouts, which made people laugh. Robin said he would assume they were philosophical propositions, but hadn't contemplated a donkey-boy as a daughter.

'Some people get horses for daughters,' said Fran.

'Hmn,' said Robin, without perfect logic or certain meaning.

Six

DIARY 23rd June, youd think it was someones
birthday. Telaphoning on the way to the knives.
The knives are quite cold. Like Granny. I am just
beside them but I have not touched the yellow
cloth even. Praps I never will and they will
always ——————————— cant write it I thougt I
wuold telaphone Christ but she was not in, just
the ringring ringring. Im glad Wendy was not
there, I dont want any one that knows any
thing becaus actuly any thing will be wrong. Ive
got dispair. (I will) I have my other trousers on
now, my genes are in the bin, how will they get
washed if Fran   ? I am sitting on my bed. I
can see down in the road. The Rennow is not
there, just its space. I took off my glasses and I
cant even see the space, but I think its just as
there. There is Mr Pattypattys beatle I can see
the red of it, and there is the mg of number 19,
orange and our space is road colour not green
like Rennow. I am thinking of who I know that
dosnt know me. I think I am really in a bit of a
pac-nic. Some things dont hapen any more, so
ever thing could not hapen any more just the

same. Robin biting my botam when I was very little, his mustach tikcled my back ever so much I cuoldnt breath. Your mothers jam. Thats Grannys plum jam, the last of your mothers jam. Wendy dosnt do that, Fran dosnt do that. Granny dosnt do that now of coarse. Grannys house was nearly small enough to see, intelagence size.

One day Grandpa was there, but not Wendy and so were we. I remeber we went to a place where I thought it was all beds, and a man in a dress said they were and they wuold get up soon. Of coarse I know what it was now, but I was little then. Actuly I knew then. But we still had the Rennow. I am being a baby. The man was a ministre and I cant remeber wether he had robes. He said Granny was a true lady, and Wendy looked frontwards, I could tell because she wanted to be one, why dosent she ask Grandpa?

'You can powder your nose,' said Robin. 'There won't be any offence taken.'

'I always did powder it,' said Fran. 'I feel different, that's all. You feel complicated enough about it all; well, so do I, don't I?'

'I don't feel complicated about anything,' said Robin. 'Once it's reduced to logical order then it's merely a matter of choice. And a choice is what's available.'

'We know who was available then,' said Fran.

It was a quarrel, Fran thinking that Robin would rather have had Wendy, if his father hadn't found her first and now had her instead of Granny.

Granny did not seem to mind. She dressed in black and had a striped cat, some geese and plum trees.

['Me and the fireside,' she said. 'I don't want any money fellows about.']

Grandpa was the money fellow, HEMPSTALL HEMPSTALL HEMPSTALL on all sorts of street corners where his shops were. He was never in them when Fran took Victoria shopping.

Victoria used to call them pram shops, because of the supermarket carts with her name on each one. There was one in Stokes Croft, quite a long way from Clifton, and Fran went there sometimes. When they went to the farm they drove even further into a town and bought groceries from HEMPSTALL HEMPSTALL HEMPSTALL there. There was only one Hempstall, Grandpa. He had his name written on the shop fronts as many times as possible. What happened was that he grew rich. Victoria thought that if you grew rich you could buy jam from the shop and didn't need Granny to make it, so you had Wendy instead. Fran tried to explain something but it was clear to Victoria what Grandpa thought.

['The up-the-valley man comes from the corner shop,' said Granny. 'Brings my bits and pieces, thank you. I'm not supporting him,' with a wag of the head meaning Grandpa and HEMPSTALL HEMPSTALL HEMPSTALL.]

But in the car, now, at Granny's house this last time, Robin said nothing more. Fran said, 'The mirrors will all be covered up today. They do that here.' She scattered powder about, snip-

49

snapped the compact shut, and dropped it into her bag. She turned round and wiped Victoria's face and hands with a sweet-smelling cold tissue out of a sachet. She took the key from the lock, and waited for Robin to get out, then slid over and got out herself. Robin was muttering about superstition, Victoria hoping it didn't mean anything she could understand.

They had had to park a little way from the house, because of other cars. They got out into wet grass on the roadside, and walked up what seemed a long way to the house.

Victoria did not expect other people to be there. There never had been others. She had never seen Grandpa there. Wendy wasn't there. She was at the songs later. Granny was not by the fire, neither was the striped cat.

'I have tried to prepare her,' said Fran. 'But I think she expects it to be just the same.'

Victoria knew it wasn't the same. She had been told too much in some ways. She wanted to find out for herself what she would think, not be told.

['Don't believe a word,' said Granny. 'Touch it with your own fingers, then you know.' It was a caterpillar, and it stung like a nettle. Granny smiled and put butter on.]

She wanted to think of climbing against that shiny black lap, to feel from there the glow of the coal fire high on the hearth, to smell the spurts of gassy smoke that came from the tar mounds behind the bars.

She wanted to stroke and smell the cat, striped as if it too had bars.

['The pair of us keep the house,' said Granny. 'In our furabouts.']

She wanted to see it stretch, and feel herself stretching with

50

it, kicking off her shoes beside it on the clothy rug, extending the claws in her toes, arching and relaxing her back, twitching her tail, and yawning.

She wanted to be sitting at Granny's tiny table for a meal, with Granny telling her to be still and not eat with both hands.

['A lady's mouth is in the middle, not by her ear,' said Granny. 'Only whispers go in a lady's ear.']

She wanted to walk in the little garden, a garden the size of her vision, one her own size, understandable.

['Nothing much should come out of her mouth,' said Granny. 'Maybe a kiss.']

She did not want these things to have stopped without notice. So she asked for Granny, who always had all these things for her, biscuits from up-the-valley, stripy sweets that Fran thought common.

['Leave one in the jar,' said Granny, 'so the next one knows where to live.']

Fran looked at Grandpa. Grandpa looked at other people. 'Well,' he said, 'all right then. Are you going up, Fran? In the room there, in bed. It's sleep.'

['Go to sleep quietly,' said Granny. 'Except the last time.']

'Not just now,' said Fran.

'Now is the time,' said Grandpa. 'You, boy?' Boy was Robin. Boy took Victoria's hand. She was going up. It was her Granny in the bed.

['I won't wake you,' said Granny in her mornings there, 'but day's come calling.']

They went through the door at the bottom of the stairs, and up to the landing. It was a little landing, and two men were

51

standing there. They had a big box between them, not the blanket box that usually stood in the alcove and camphored the air when it was opened.

Robin hesitated, not sure what to do. He was not used to men on the landing of his mother's house, and having to walk round that sort of box.

'In the room, sir,' said one of the men. 'You'll be the last, will you? You are very like her, you must be the son.'

'That's right,' said Robin.

'Affirmative,' said Victoria. 'Boy.'

['Don't agree too soon,' said Granny. 'You might disagree even sooner one day. Give yourself time.']

'Hush,' said Robin. 'My wife isn't coming up.'

'We're going to have a job on, believe me,' said the man, chattily. 'But I think we got two lads from the farm coming to help.' No one had gossiped on the landing before.

'We'll be a moment, only,' said Robin, looking despairingly at Victoria, hoping she would go downstairs. She was not going downstairs. It was her Granny, not Robin's.

'Very peaceful, she is,' said the second man. 'Lovely old lady. Dignified. Well-known. I'll step in with you, you'd like that better, wouldn't you?'

Robin edged his way round the big box, hoping there was not enough space in the room beyond for Victoria. For him. There was.

Victoria looked into the box. It was lined inside, like a cradle, but empty. Not even corrugated cardboard. For her, cradles had dolls, but she was surprised to find the doll for this cradle in Granny's bed. She knew it was Granny, and she knew Granny was dead, but the ideas did not come together very well at all. How could this big still doll be Granny? and how could it be anyone else? It was a false Granny, but made out of the real one.

'Day's come calling,' she said, knowing there are other days than those upon earth and land and Welsh hills.

Robin felt some of the same things. 'Great God,' he said, 'they've powdered her nose. She never did anything like that herself in her life.'

'It's always done,' said the man who had come in with them. 'Of course it has to be. It is a special occasion for everybody.'

['You'll know the best day when it comes,' said Granny. 'It's like all the others, special through, but nothing like the day they killed the pig.']

'Should I, you know, touch her?' said Robin.

'I seen it done many a time,' said the man. 'Farewell kiss and so on.'

'Mmn,' said Robin. He stayed looking for a while. For him there was no read-out from his mother now; her eyes were closed.

Victoria climbed up on the hard edge of the bed. She had sat by Granny just so, early in the morning, when they had all come to stay in the other tiny bedroom. Granny had her best lace-edged pillowslip under her head. Victoria put her head down on the pillow beside Granny's, and looked at the profile of her face, with the blurred window beyond. Granny went on looking at the ceiling with her shut eyes.

['You look so peaceful,' said Granny, 'I'll leave you without your breakfast, unless you are greedy enough to get up.']

Granny was cold. No one had said that to Victoria. She rolled off the bed.

53

'That's pretty, then,' said the man. He smiled at Victoria, but she was busy trying to put together all the pictures of Granny: by the fire and about the house; not being anywhere at all; being a doll in a box; being dead but still herself; being warm always. There was too much taking-away from one person.

['It's the wind in the chimney,' said Granny. 'Saying nothing, goodness, filling our lives. Put on some more wood, keep the wind the other end.']

On the way downstairs they met the two Welsh boys from the farm. They were trying to look solemn, in best clothes and with smart hats, not their caps.

'Helloo,' they said, coming up the stairs two at a step, bent over and devout. 'Sad day, Mr Robin, for you. Awkward old place, these stairs, izzenet. Helloo litt-el one, it is sad about your nana. We are going to carry her very gentle.'

Victoria went to sit by the fire. She was Granny for a time, by her own hearth, but her feet did not reach the rug.

['I stobbed that rug,' said Granny. 'That's the word; and see, here's a grey jacket of his, underfoot; and that's a red skirt, long ago.' And she was long ago herself for a moment, stirring the flattened cloth with a black shoe, treading down the past.]

After a time the box came downstairs and out of the door. Whatever Granny was had now gone from the house. There was no one left for Victoria to be. She got down from the chair and went in the Renault again to a chapel. Wendy was there, looking a bit forgotten.

They followed the box inside for songs, and then outside. There were yellow flowers in the grass, and there were transparent, glistening flowers of dew as well, leaning over her shoes

54

and kissing Victoria's ankles cold. That cold was life for dew; the other cold had been death in Granny.

When they came to the side of the grave someone patted her head. The straight-sided grave was at first only a hole to Victoria, with nothing of interest in it. But in a little while the two Welsh boys lowered Granny there on straps, in her covered cradle. Down she went, in all her good clothes, and earth was knocked on her. Victoria knew she would not like the dirtiness of that.

· ['Walk in anything,' said Granny, putting Victoria's shoes outside, 'you got to walk everywhere to get somewhere.']

No one else thought about such things. They seemed to forget Granny straight away.

'She'll be all right, Queen,' said Grandpa. He often called Victoria Queen.

The Welsh boys grinned out loud now, not quietly as they had done on the stairs. They unbuttoned their waistcoats and pulled their ties off before they got from the little graveyard out into the road. One of them carried Granny's striped cat in a box, going to a new home at the farm. It had been taken six times, and always walked back to a cold hearth.

Robin locked the cottage door, gave the key to his father, and walked by himself for a time.

'He thinks it's logic,' said Fran. 'But it's sense.'

Victoria looked back and saw all the beds in that field, boards at the heads and frames laid out, and the dewy grass grown over them.

In one corner two men were slowly at work with spades. They had known Granny. She was not alone, but among friends.

['Talk, we have, and laughter,' she said, 'the fire listening and the cat forgetting.']

What Victoria remembered most about the day happened on the way to the chapel, when they met three people on horseback, who stopped riding and took off their hats while the black car with Granny in it went by. A girl's hair fell down golden all over her back in the sunshine, and that was Victoria's figure for a resurrection.

['Waking up next day,' said Granny. 'That's the big surprise. Sit up, get up, it doesn't come again.']

Except the last time, thought Victoria. That comes again for ever. Then she had a fleeting thought about taking the cat back to Bristol, and put it aside until that last day. I'd take it, she thought. Even if I couldn't. God will be less trouble than Robin.

Then they went to the farm again and had a big meal. Victoria saw the egg sandwiches being made, with hard-boiled eggs and HEMPSTALL HEMPSTALL HEMPSTALL mayonnaise. The Welsh boys ate a whole plate of them, and put on more mayonnaise, a serious sort of shovelling, more vigorous than the two old friends still at the graveyard.

Seven

DIARY I know I have got an intalect, because of
not being a houseflie or other object, however if
Robin says that lies are evedence of weak
intalect then I have not got any. I have been
telling lies to myself, but it is malfuntcion. The
boys name is Paul. But he calls me Victorial so I
shuold call him Paw?? Robin and Fran have
gone out in a peculiar way. I think they have
died out. I have an (~~insin~~) (~~incinct~~) inctinct that
they are (~~exci~~) (~~ecxst~~) exctinct and I shall have
to dry the knives. I shall have to be in dispair
while I dry the knives for ever and ever omen. It
is dispair of wondreing what hapened to
perants. Praps I am still drying the knives from
the time before, another 23rd June, nearly
midsumer. Where ever I think, it is all there
before. Like a fostle in the (~~memery memary~~)
mind. If I had forgoten it until now of coarse it
is wurse this time, if I new what it was. It is
dredful and wrong. It is'nt all imagenery, it is'nt
just an (~~idael~~) (~~ideal~~) idea. But it is like being
not real atall, it was realer when I smelt my
knees. I shuold not of gone riding. I have to

57

take the horse back. I do not like a horse, I
think I hate it. I hate its head leaning over. I did
not dry the knives, I came in my room again
and got my list about horses. They did not hear
me.

Perhaps they had not spoken, when things of the same sort
happened before.

'All the way to Weston,' Robin had said, very long ago.
Weston-super-Mare; Robin nearly pleased at getting anywhere.

'We set out to go to Wells,' said Fran, in small writing but
underlined, the chalk nearly breaking. She was in the back of
the car, stretched out better there. She was pale after being in
hospital. She was sad as well, so far away in thinking about
other things that nothing close-to worried her. Usually she
was patient about arriving at the wrong town after a drive, but
today she pointed out what had happened and went back to
other thoughts. Robin, at this time, was short-tempered with
the whole world. He was always ready to be exasperated with
anyone and anything, anywhere; now he was out to get the
wrong thing said to him, the wrong thing done, but actually
getting to the wrong place on his own was not the same as
being sent there. He was not good at reading the signs, though
he could see them. Victoria might have been better at the signs,
but she could not see them at all.

At Weston Fran had to sit up and direct them to a car park.
Victoria got out and led the car to an empty place. She could
see empty places pretty well, but she had left her glasses at
home, so she parked the car in a gateway, Fran not noticing and

Robin not thinking of what was going on, now he had successfully got somewhere.

In the end, after the man had come along, Fran had to get in the car and drive it about, but it made her sadder than she already was, herself an empty place, a useless gateway, colourless like road.

It was a warm sunny day. The tide was out and the mud was up. They walked down to the beach and sat on deck chairs. No one came along to charge them so Robin could not relax. Fran closed her eyes. Victoria did the same. Robin sat up and watched for the attendant, ready to pay.

With shut eyes Victoria could smell the beach (starfish), the chair (pink teddies in a tent), the sun-tan oil of other people (fried), and hear beyond the people and the gulls (small-child) the distant lap of the sea (iodine from HHH IN-STORE PHARMACY on a scratch), casting on and casting off the lace stitches of foam.

Her hand felt the grit of desert at her fingertips (and an ice-lolly wrapper rustled against her thumb). If she could slide into the sandiness of the sand and the sea-ness of the sea and the sun-ness of the day, she could be separate and happy.

Beside her Fran began to sob in the sunlight. Victoria listened far away, with eyes closed: night in the further world.

'Is there anything I can do?' said Robin.

'Oh no,' said Fran. 'A tissue, if you have one. I don't mean to cry, but I can't help it.'

'I hope it was all right to come out,' said Robin.

'I didn't want to come out,' said Fran. 'I didn't want to come to Weston if I did come out. I don't like it here, and I wouldn't like it at Wells, but I wouldn't have liked it at home either, so it's just my state at the moment, and we can't do anything about it but learn to live with it.'

'It isn't anybody's fault,' said Robin.

'No,' said Fran. 'And we couldn't do anything about it if it were. But I expect we are all sorry about different things, so will you let me go to sleep now?' In the end she had turned disagreeable, and there was nothing more for Robin to say, and nothing more for Victoria to hope she had not heard. Why should the hospital make Fran particularly miserable, when she had been looking forward to going in?

The desert sand came to Victoria's fingers again. It was warm on top and rapidly cooler below, and more and more dense. Then camels came walking by. She opened her eyes when she heard the solid slow trudge. She opened them at the sun, and was blinded by all she could see as well as by what she could not see. By staring away to one side she saw the shape of a movement, going along like a table. It was donkeys. Since they had been thinking of Wells as they came, donkeys had not been in her mind.

'Robin,' she said, 'give me all my money, please.'

'I'll buy you an ice-cream,' he said.

'Thanks,' said Victoria. 'I'll have that as well, but in money. There's donkeys.'

'Donkeys?' said Robin, obviously thinking about donkey-flavoured ice-cream. It was the sort of thinking that had brought them to Weston, with Robin going to a place beginning with WE. If he was talking about ice-cream, so was Victoria, he assumed, whatever flavour she wanted.

'Donkey riding,' said Victoria. 'Before they go out of sight.'

'You've got a horse,' said Robin. 'You had your fill of donkey rides in Greece, that island.'

'We aren't there any more,' said Victoria.

'No,' said Robin. 'But you have a horse of your own, which you could have ridden this afternoon, but you chose to come out with us. You don't need a donkey ride as well.'

Sometimes it is not possible to say exactly what you think. Victoria wanted to say that if she had had a donkey not a horse, she would now be riding it, or brushing it, talking to it, or carrying it about: she would be loving it. She could not love a horse. But when it was given to her she had not been able to say anything against having it. Sometimes it is not possible to think any right thing.

'Let her, Robin,' said Fran.

'It'll be fair if she doesn't,' said Robin.

'I'm not talking about equity,' said Fran. 'I'm talking about equitation.' It was not a joke but a quarrel.

'Come on,' said Victoria. 'I want to ride all the time.'

'I don't see . . .' said Robin, when he had caught up with her. 'I don't see why it takes you twenty seconds to be ready to ride a donkey when it took you an hour and a half last Saturday to get ready to ride your own horse once round a field. Once only. That's not a very big use.'

'It's a very big horse,' said Victoria. 'I can hardly see the field from it.'

'Nonsense,' said Robin.

But what she said was true; her sight began to decay at ground-level. 'If I could see through it,' she said, 'I wouldn't be able to.'

'Don't begin making jokes,' said Robin. 'Truth is hard enough to come by without making jokes.'

'It isn't a joke,' said Victoria. 'Sand is getting in my sandals. That isn't a joke either. So wait a minute.'

She had four rides, and three walks up and down with the donkey boy, and an extra ride up the beach on Robin's back.

'You're getting too big for this,' he said. But she put her hands round his head and pulled at his moustache.

'It is your bit,' she said. He spluttered under her sandpapery hands.

At the deck chairs Fran was sitting with her eyes closed, and in front of her was the attendant, wondering what to do, and whether he had made her cry. When he asked for money Fran had dripped tears but not opened her eyes.

'I never said a word of any offence,' said the man. 'Is she all right?'

'A bit down at present,' said Robin. 'Convalescent now, nothing functional, just in the programming.'

'You get some funny things on the radio,' said the man. He issued three tickets and went away.

'Cheaper to sit on a donkey,' said Robin.

They sat for a while longer, and then went home. Robin had to give up driving near Bristol, and Fran took over. He would never have got them home through the town.

Victoria sat beside Fran and thought of something that was a poem and not a poem, about donkeys. It was a poem because it felt like one, and not a poem because of a shortage of words. But in time she wrote down the essence of it, when she came across the words that fitted it. It came out as a list, written down a page, showing that a donkey was one set of things, and a horse another:

A donkey is sweet,
    A horse is intemperate.
A donkey is docile,
    A horse is wild.
A donkey is hardy,
    A horse is delicate.
A donkey is small,
    A horse is huge.
A donkey is stubborn,
    A horse is headstrong.
A donkey is patient,
    A donkey is sensitive,
A horse is senseless,
    A donkey is beloveable.

She came back from Weston smelling of donkey and tasting salt when she licked her lips, on the pencil between words.

'I can taste it too,' said Fran. 'But it's tears for me. I'm sorry I'm in this silly way, and you mustn't take any notice.' And the silly way she was in made her go to bed as soon as they got home.

Victoria went to bed after Fran was asleep, the day ending the wrong way up for her, and sat against the window while the light came in, drawing donkeys and naming them, Hugo, May, Carlos, Aphrodite, Jenny, Gold, on and on until the pasture of the page was full, and then more and more until the light was gone, and the last hundred unborn and unnamed.

In the morning the sheet was scribble, the writing here and there neat but trodden over by wilder and wilder donkeys and more names, until there was only a stampede of pencil, a wilderness of asses, thistles in paradise.

Eight

DIARY It is some of what hapened before, some other midsumer, perhaps thats rigth. I am thinking it I am not writeing it down, I cant get it to the paper, why dosnt paper come with it all printed on like news. I surpose we wuoldnt read it, we dont want to know that. But Robin says a fact is a fact, however he is wrong. ~~Robin is wrong~~. ROBIN IS WRONG. Things arent the same, its what I think about things makes them what they are. Its where it is in my intalect. I have a diferent intelagence than Robin. May be they went shoping in the middle of drying the knives, well for them they did that but if they arent here when I come in, why? He wuold forget the bit that he isnt in, and thats the bit I am in. It means an awful thing has hapened. I wont ask Mr Pattypatty.

I am now sitting on my bed. The toilet sistine is dropping drops inside every second of time. I am sitting on my bed again but inbetween I have been to telaphone Christ again but she was engadged. I cant think of any one I know. That boy would be out. I know his name is

Paul. Robin has two names for them all, one is Lilliputains for the universey which is the intalectul ones, and the shop and bussiness ones are Bolians. Bolians say L on the ends of words, like ammonial says the womon at the shop, so Paul is a Bolian, he calls me Victorial. I think Angela Creasy prefect is his sister. His card has a picture of a merygorounde on it.

I tell lies for show-off, I told him one at Xtmas, but it was true, boneles turkey roast that day, but we went to the farm not long after and Robin and Wendy got lost all afternoon and Fran was wild because of Robin being roten soft on Wendy and calling me after her. Why wuold he send me a picture of a merygorounde? I didn't really see it until today, I wasnt thinking of it. I will never buy a boneless turkey roast for my children, in fact children are a bad idea(l). I don't know which word I mean. If Grandpa and Wendy had some they wuold be my aunt or uncle. (Fran has stopped) I cuold tel if I went up in the secret room. I shuold not of gone there and rode the horse to death when I was so big then I would not of seen the cradle cot. There is something they do not explain. Paul has no telaphone number on his card, besides he is out going towards Nailsea I saw him at Abots Lea. He had sandwiches at Xtmas and I know he wuold not tell a lie.

'A beautiful day for anything,' said Mum. They were driving across the Downs in Tina. 'I don't mind a picnic now and then, but I'm a town girl at heart, and if there's sunshine I'm happiest to see it like it is now, on all the houses round the Downs. The Downs are country enough for me; that and the seaside now and then.'

'But Christmas day with sandwiches,' said Angela.

'Well then?' said Dad.

'No, no, I don't mean I don't like it,' said Angela. 'I mean it's a strange thing for the day, and we aren't doing it for any silly reason like fun, but for something serious. That's proper, is that. And today there's no traffic about, so Tiny Wee hasn't started to turn pale.'

'All that chocolate before breakfast,' said Dad, 'do steady the stomach marvellous.'

Something steadied the stomach until they were well across the bridge. Dad was able to stop the car and let Tiny Wee run about on the road edge for a while, but nothing happened.

''Tis like taking the dog out,' said Dad. 'She won't oblige. Well, we'll just go on. We're used to that, I think.'

So they went on. They had come to the field, and Paul was opening the gate, with Tiny Wee riding on it. This last thing was enough. She gave the world the delayed performance. She was exceedingly angry when they laughed at her. Dad drove on up the field, Paul latched the gate back. Mum looked in the hedge and saw the sparrows running and said, 'I'll bet they're glad they aren't turkeys.'

Martin and Angela ran after the car, stamping like children on the other's shadow, rare wildness for either of them.

'Too much gate,' said Tiny Wee, licking her lips. 'More lovely chocky.'

When they came up to the barn the doors were open and Dad inside looking at the drawings. "Tis a fine day,' he said, 'we could pull all the trailers out, but if we do we have them to put back again later. Remember it isn't like summer work, dark so early. Twenty minutes to pull them out, forty to push them back. It might be an idea to get some of the back trailers out to the front.'

To anyone else, Mum's next remark would have sounded like nonsense. 'If you brought some coal and some Christmas carols,' she said.

'Music,' said Tiny Wee. 'Book music.'

They all liked the music. They knew what to do to get it. Trailer seven had to be located and worked forward. It meant moving the other trailers, but not very far.

Trailer seven stood like a canvas drum out in the field ten minutes later. It was the heaviest trailer, with four wheels and sturdy legs to be wound down. Paul went in under it and pulled out the chimney. Last year's soot fell out on his fingers.

This'll be a summery-feeling Christmas, he thought. It'll be all right. We think of Christmas at home, eating and watching television, but it's fine to be out here working at the same thing together. He thought how he had given the thing to the girl in the church that morning, the photograph of it set up on the Downs. Last winter he had worked on it, as they all had, but he had not had the same thoughts; there had been no girls, no girl, in the world. Even Tiny Wee had been something you carried about. But now there was Wendy, or Victoria, and no

68

explanation of why she added so much to his life, and took away so much as well. The soot fell into his palm. Last year that soot, the whole ride, had been nearly all the world to him. Now more than mere chemical character had gone from the dry grains dusting his hand.

The others had been pulling the canvas away. Paul crouched where he was, underneath, having his thoughts while the others' legs maypoled about the trailer. It was the centre trailer of the whole machine, the one on which all stood and on which all depended, and which drove all. This trailer had taken Dad seven long years of work, piece by piece, shape by shape, a nut and a bolt at a time, until it was ready. Those years had been half Paul's childhood. That's what it is, he thought; dust in the palm of your hand. He blew it away and came out. Dad was already climbing up on the platform and calling for the hose. There was a trough with a tap at the barn. The hose came with Martin, and Dad took the end and plunged it into the water box. The hose stiffened as the water came through it.

Paul went up the other side with the chimney. Dad put a firelighter in the hearth, and a bundle of sticks, then dropped in coal piece by piece. He put in his hand, lit the firelighter, and closed the fire-door. He stayed to watch the water coming in, then closed the tap and reeled the hose away.

That was all that could be done just now. Dad was tempted and so was Paul, to dust and polish, but that would be waste work: now they had the day's tasks to do, while the boiler heated the water to steam.

'Book music,' said Tiny Wee.

'Some families, I hear,' said Angela, 'get a radio in the car. The quaint old-fashioned things.'

'Eccentric,' said Paul. 'Off centre.' But he thought a different thing, that there were many centres to each person, more and more as time goes on. Tiny Wee, skipping up and down on the spot, has fewer centres than Martin, who is waiting to do what comes next, a very sensible boy; and I myself have at least one other centre no one knows about, probably not even the girl. I don't know what kind of centre it is, but things have to go round it. Martin hasn't any centre like that, and once I hadn't either; even half a year ago. And Angela must have more centres again. But it is hard to tell with her. And Mum, she has us for a centre most of all, but we are all close together: perhaps Angela is waiting for a cluster of centres like that. Mum has no other centres. But Dad; he has his work at the Post Office, and he has this machine, and he has us, and that's all one again. Is it possible for all one's centres to get into balance, to be a stable nucleus, without pulling and taking away from each other?

Now he set his hand to what there was to do. He did it willingly; he wanted to do nothing else. But minute after minute there came a message from his heart, a flutter under the ribs, that said he was thinking of the girl.

'Yes, that's what she's called,' said Angela. 'I meant to tell you.'

'What?' said Paul. 'Who?'

'You were muttering to yourself,' said Angela. 'You said Victoria.'

'I didn't,' said Paul. But the word, the name, was inside him and filling him, so that he could not be sure it was not forming outside him too, as speech.

'Oh yes,' said Angela. 'I expect you're in love.'

'Is that it?' said Paul. 'It's something.'

'Who's that, then?' said Mum. They were moving her boxes into the warm place at the back of the barn. 'This fat little girl in the third form,' said Angela, 'took Paul's fancy. Victoria's her name in the lists, but she gets called Wendy.'

'Like Marion gets called Tiny Wee,' said Mum. 'You can take messages for them both, Angela. Paul and your one.'

'Not to form three,' said Angela. 'He does his own fetch and carry.'

'Where does she live to, Paul?' asked Mum, with a stranger's companionable smile.

'Steam's getting up,' said Paul. He was not referring to any internal state of his, but to the centre truck outside with the boiler on it. There was a damp hissing and spluttering from it. He went across to close the valve down and let the pressure build up. Not much pressure was needed for music. She lives, he thought. She does not live to. That will never be her speaking.

A quarter of an hour later the concert started. Dad had the books of music in their lockers. They were long folded strips, reinforced with scrim, and punched with holes so that the machinery could read the note to play. It began with a piece called 'The Waltz March'. Mum said it was the three-legged parade, but for the rest of them it was fit for dancing, and had an air of Christmas about it.

'Keep the pressure about forty,' said Dad. 'I'm going on with trailer three. We got those irons to loose and paint and fix up tight again, and we have the platform to check. Six months and we're on the road.'

Mum went back to her warm room, after a short waltz-march dance with Martin. Back there she had a contrivance beside the gas panel-heater. No one was allowed in to ask what it was, but Paul's guess to himself was to do with ovens. Dad said he knew nothing about it; she must have been doing her own inventing. Paul thought Dad had invented it, without any guarantees about how it would work.

But something was happening. Loosening bolts, with the sunshine on him in the doorway of the barn, and the music pouring out and filling the field, Paul felt more than the smell of oil in his nostrils. There was something more than sandwich round the turkey, it seemed.

Outside, Martin put on 'Carolina', then 'Turkish Delight', which seemed appropriate, and then the book with no title, known only to be composed by someone whose printed name had decomposed to '. . pig . .'.

Mum, left to herself, had been busier than anyone could be in a barn with no kitchen, no dining room, nothing of any domestic nature at all. At the end of several renderings of '. . pig . .' she had come out from her warm place, and announced lunch. Dad said it was early yet, but Angela reminded him of the day. He wiped his hands and came. He said he had got so far in what he was doing he didn't want to stop, and if it was the resurrection at the last day he'd want to get things right before going; and he said he felt he ought not to drag them all out this day of the year just so that they would help him.

Mum said they had discussed that long ago, and were quite happy. Dad however, had to go to the car now, and bring out an extra round of presents he had scraped up, because he felt he ran everything for his own benefit, his own interests, and they might not be to everyone else's benefit and taste.

Paul thought, the centres he is going round are not quite so tightly together as I think. He did not know whether to be pleased at that or sorry, since being too smooth-running might leave one unable to do fresh things and having many separate centres might be too uncomfortable.

Dad gave him a new music stand, for which he was glad and sorry again. Now he would not have to walk up to Angela's school two days a week, which saved him trouble, but it deprived him of one of his chances of glimpsing Victoria.

But now he had spoken to her, distant glimpses were perhaps of little use. He would have no longer the opportunity and joy of chance encounter.

After that there were ordinary presents, from Dad and Mum and each other and people outside, and Mum's thoughtful idea of carrier bags to keep things in.

After that there was a small packet each, containing a paper napkin, a cracker, a fizzy drink, a straw, and a bundle of knives, forks and spoons. Mum had help from Paul to lift away the contrivance that was some sort of oven, and inside it was a roasted turkey, surrounded by all the vegetables that it must have been impossible to cook there at all, flanked by stuffing, and appearing in clouds of steam and gushes of heat.

'Look at thiccy thur thang turkey before my very eyes,' said Dad. 'Well, that do beat all. Imaginary that is, I don't believe it, I can't.'

But he had to carve it, all the same. Before he had finished, Tiny Wee had her bottle of fizz open, drunk it, and with a great

73

grin given the biggest belch anyone had heard (they said admiringly). 'We don't need no steam organ,' said Dad. 'We've got a machine that do play that piece by Pig right off, no trouble at all.'

After lunch the fire in the boiler had gone out. Paul drained the water away. When they all felt enough digestion had taken place they moved trailer seven indoors again.

'We haven't done so bad,' said Dad. 'All we could have wished for, today, I reckon. Some lunch that was, Mother.'

'Sandwiches tomorrow,' said Mum

At least not a boneless turkey roast, thought Paul. I wonder what it is like to be that girl. Victoria. Does she know she is present with me so much that at times I must carefully think of other things in order not to embarrass her? Can she know that? How can she not know it? Shall we get back in time for me to walk that way for a little while?

Before they got into the car Angela drew him aside. 'I'll tell you something you don't know,' she said. 'I found it out at school. Mum and Dad don't know, and you don't. You ought to know, but I don't think they should. It's a fact of life, but not a biological one.'

'What's it about?' said Paul. But he knew whom it would be about.

'Not her,' said Angela. 'About you, and me, and all of us. What's her name, really, in the end?'

'Victoria,' said Paul. 'She did . . . she told me.' He had stopped his natural expression, 'She did tell I', because it was no longer appropriate, for reasons he knew of but hardly understood.

'But you don't know what you say,' said Angela. 'You're a proper Bristolian. You say "Victorial".'

'Do I?' said Paul. 'That be, that is, her name?'

It took Angela five minutes to show him what he was doing, and he left her with clean lips, able to say the word clear, but able to hear his parents putting an 'l' on each word that would take it, like ideal for idea, or areal for area; and he knew there was nothing he must say about that for ever. That he had already known it before Angela spoke only made him a traitor to his upbringing. More was taken away than was given: anything more, any replacements, would have to be found and earned, as acts of greater treachery. But those purified lips were tainted with treachery and rejection.

At the bridge he had himself put down. He walked in the darkness of the evening, along the streets at the side of the gorge, longing to see, only to see her, but he did not.

He went home over the dry Downs, saying the name without the 'l', pushing his tongue forward as Angela had taught him, as they had taught her at school. He knew from the few words Victoria and her mother had spoken that they would not use the Bristol 'l', but would notice if he did, and be in turn unable to explain away what they felt about it.

How can anything of mine be made less by what she thinks of it? he asked himself. He knew that it must be so, but it hurt that he might not be considerate enough by nature, in language or manners or other matters; it hurt him to think it necessary to change towards things he had not learned at home, and could not. What is there good, he wondered, about so painful a love? Is it always anguish, in spite of being inevitable?

And there were other things.

'You said "hurfwah",' said Mrs Anderson once, when science was being practical. The memory came risingly into Paul's mind, bitter and rich. 'You *mean* what you have written, "earth wire".'

Paul looked at his ignition diagram. He heard his own speech against his written words, insulated from their meanings by his tongue.

In the dusk a tear of no significance, of no outward showing, starred a street lamp, agony upon agony; and his very footsteps trailed him, thick and indistinct as any other utterance. He led them home.

Nine

DIARY I have telaphoned Christ again, I cuold hardly speak I am cold I think. It is a warme day outside, summertime. I think it is the house. I do not know wether Christ was any help.

RING RING, RING RING

MOTHER OF CHRIST hello.

ME is Christ in please.

MOTHER OF CHRIST I-ll get him.

ME thinking, she all ways says that.

CHRIST hello Wend what did you want?

ME not a lot.

CHRIST thats good I havent got much. {Luagh} What are you doing?

ME nothing theyve all gone out.

CHRIST you lucky thing I wish mine wuold there isnt any thing to do. Did you visit your relitiv?

ME yes.

This is acounting for haveing a cecret horse I am unproud of. Pink.

CHRIST youve got every thing. You can help in the shop if you want, thatted be good

She means HHH, she thinks there is only one not a chain like Grannys old toilet.

CHRIST continuedly, I wish we had a shop, not just my dad working in an office, boreing.

ME I dont know where they went.

CHRIST it dosnt matter, you can lay on your bed and put your feet out the (~~windew~~) window who cares.

ME Ive got to go now.

CHRIST well see you, Wend, trah.

Its like talking to a hole in a wall, she dosnt hear but I cuold hardly speak I didnt say much. If I cuold of— The telaphone went again at me. It was saying,

TELAPHONE this is Christs mother is that Wendy.

ME yes.

MOTHER OF CHRIST youre all alone arnt you? Is every thing all right Christ wondred.

ME yes Im fine.

MOTHER OF will mummy and daddy be back soon?

ME yes.

MOTHER OF CHRIST on and on a bit about being quite sure.

ME mummy and daddy will be back soone, ta, ring off.

Fran gets wild about Ta but goes mad about mummy and daddy, it isnt them, mummy and daddy, praps they arnt my perants, I migt be

the (~~duaghter~~) daugther of a royalty praps I am
the son of a royalty, no, but I am called from a
queen, I wondred why Grandpa called me that.
If she rings again I have plenty of paper, Robin
gets it from the universery computors, he used
to say it came from the zoo it was elaphents
bumf and it was also a joake. One side is white,
the other has blue lines and messeges from
computors in big letters. This one says RUN 70
TRACE 70 THRO 48 ERROR CANCEL REENTER,
on the back of it. Once it had put IS THERE ANY
BODY THERE QUERY. Well there was me but
that dosnt count, or I cuold send a messege
back saying DO NOT SHOWT use little letters,
or I cuold say I was an extra terrace
intelagence. Once Grandpa or Wendy gave me
this folding thing a J-Cub ladder, a lot of
dominoe things joined together. You pick it up
by a dominoe and the others fall to the
(~~bottam~~) botom botham but nothing hapened
at all it is an elusion, there is some cecret to it.

Computor paper is like that, but without the
cecret. I can lift it up and read both sides, like
zigazag. It has got my DIARY on one side and
the computors on the other. I am saying IS
THERE SOMBODY HERE QUERY and they come
back and say you were showting, Vict. I wish
they were here to ignore me. I am good at that.
I am not good at being left behind, that is
difarent. They wuold not mind if they got

sombody else. That is what they are

I have got to go out again because of the horse. But I do not like the horse, if I say I do that is not the normality of me, but them, they want a difarent normal than me VICTORIA WENDY HEMPSTALL

I broke the law. I do lies in the DIARY but I brake the law out on the bridge. They dont know where I live, praps they have seen me in the Rennow, and they cuold find that. But it isnt out there now they wont know I am here. But I definately broke the law, it just wasnt my foult. The horse isnt any where near. Where are Robin and Fran, it is hours now. Where did they go in the middle of washupping and the knives in the yellow cloth. They wuoldnt of gone any where but they must of. I wuold of gone with them. I can go any where I went with Robin to the universery once to the computors when Fran was working. Robin was confusced.

Fran worked once a week during holidays. She worked all days during the term, leaving two weeks at Christmas and two at Easter for family. In the summer holiday, which was a month, Victoria went to the farm for a fortnight, and Fran had holiday herself for the two other weeks of that month and for a week when Victoria was at the farm. The day Victoria now remembered was one of the once-a-week ones. Victoria had stayed in by herself during the morning, just a couple of hours, with Mr Paterson downstairs ready to hear if she called out. She had not called out. Robin had come back and they had eaten lunch together.

After it they walked down to the University. Victoria thought they would go in the tower at the top of Park Street. That was the University tower, and she thought they should be there, the whole University in it, apparent and visible.

'No,' said Robin. 'They keep the gorilla in there, and the skeletons of the governors until they die, and then they appoint them.'

'I think you are making a joke,' said Victoria.

'Only irony,' said Robin.

'But it isn't true,' said Victoria. 'You say if it isn't true it's a joke and jokes are wrong because they are not true.'

'If we hurry,' said Robin, after thinking for a moment what to say, 'we can go in and look at the gorilla and the . . .'

'And the what?' said Victoria.

'The rest of the things,' said Robin. 'The gorilla is the logical one, but it hasn't done him much good, any more than it has me.'

Victoria wanted to fill up the walk with as much as possible, to go a swift smelling tasting touching gazing trip through a few shops on the way. Robin had to say No before they had left the house, No when they got down into Victoria Square, No when they came to the end of Whiteladies Road, No when they saw the shops, No when they came to the first doorway, and had to hold her sleeve at the second door, her arm at the third, and both arms at the fourth. They all belonged to one shop.

'Aggressive actions,' he said, 'that's me slapping you, follow a simple curve. You do enough things to make me angry and I'll fetch you one, do you hear?'

'Going through a simple shop,' said Victoria, 'follows a simple curve, zoom, zoom, zoom, zoom, and a couple of rides in the lift. It's not hard work.'

'We haven't time,' said Robin. 'Straight lines are shorter than curves, so we'll go straight past.'

They went past, not very straight, but Victoria was wanting things to happen on the way there and on the way back, and when they were there as well.

They did not get down to the tower or the museum. They turned left up the hill, and in a building there somewhere Robin found the computer room he wanted. It had no windows, but Victoria could tell from its shape that it was standing in the open air and wasn't a cave. It had white light in it, and it was neither hot nor cold but something artificial between the two, another kind of heating altogether. It had a smell of machines, and the sound of them as well, whirring and singing, and a sharp rippling noise. Victoria was sure that noise was banks of computer paper being perforated and folded. She found herself reflected in a glass panel with a little twitching machine behind it. It was running a paper frill through itself. No one else was taking any notice. Victoria looked at herself. She had white bands of light down her eyes; the fluorescent tubes were filling her glasses: she could see, but her reflection was blinded.

'Good afternoon, Dr Hempstall,' said a woman who was walking about among the machines. 'We think your program is ready to run. Are you conversant with the series 20 machines?'

'Not very well,' said Robin. 'It's surprising you still have these oldies. It's not so much that I have to do the work myself, more that I think I ought to know the practical side of it.'

'Well, Doctor, it's a pity to use running time on mistakes, when we have so many calls on it,' said the woman, gently waving a magic pencil to keep the troublesome Dr Hempstall in order. Fran did it with one eyebrow, one eyelash.

'It is clearly within my rights,' said Robin.

'Then I'll leave you to it,' said the woman. 'With an apology for being out of date.' She paused by a chair and console to show Robin where to go.

She looked at Victoria, decided that nothing could be done about such problems, went to her desk and did thoughtful things very accurately turning her head like a bird. She had a white coat and a pink scarf and no jokes, Victoria was sure. Not like Robin, who disapproved, but this lady could not understand they existed.

'You see,' said Robin, 'fiddly fiddly fiddly, little empires, little compartments. The computer is a pure creative tool, something I should be able to use without their help, or without inter-ference from commercial organisations. Well, I'll see how it goes.'

It went first with a flashing red light. A man came and consulted with Robin, and then seemed to take over the work. Victoria stood by her reflection and watched Robin, and watched the machine in the case making and rolling its paper frill. She found a box under the machine, and proved that the small white paper discs in it were holes, and that what anyone else would think were holes in the paper frill were part of the air round about, not holes: the holes were down in the box below.

Robin was not doing well. After his red light he sat there unable to do anything for a long time while his terminal printed out page after page of stuff he did not want to see. He had to go and get help to have it stopped.

Victoria noted that the sharp rippling noise was the print heads whizzing out the pages.

'I've accessed the wrong materials,' said Robin, when he had had his turn. 'I think I've wasted computer time. How was your time?'

'I should have brought my own computer,' said Victoria. 'I didn't have anything to do.'

'We'll go and get a cup of tea,' said Robin.

'Something not tea,' said Victoria.

'Anything,' said Robin. 'I should have my own terminal, not have to come down here. I should be able to use it without being an expert.'

They went to the students' refectory for a cup of tea. Neither of them was a student, but that did not matter.

'How do they know we can come in?' said Victoria.

'They don't,' said Robin. 'To them we're just holes in a tea-bag.'

'Jokes again,' said Victoria. She saved up the holes in the paper tape for some apter occasion.

They went along the cafeteria line with a tray. Robin had coffee, something he often referred to as a cup of tea, without ever drinking tea. Victoria had a flattish fizzy orange drink.

'They say this place serves the best breakfast in town,' said

Robin. 'Sunday morning is the time, open as usual but no one about. But it would be more trouble, in the end, to come all the way down here, than get it for ourselves.'

'In our nighties,' said Victoria.

'Oh no, properly dressed down here,' said Robin. 'Ten minutes more, and we'll go down and meet Fran.'

Victoria did not want to leave. A huge student in the line was eating a hamburger before he paid for it. She wanted to watch for ever and imagine the beauty of it. He finished one, and then slid back down the line and took another. He bit at it three times and it was gone. Victoria longed to eat like that, three bites like a dragon.

When they left, the student was on his fourth hamburger and the passing line was used to him, like a rock in its way. He was more than a hole in a tea-bag; he was the bag itself.

Ten

DIARY I can tell I have been in riding lesson
today (23rd), when I get up and sit down
because some riding is a sort of bounsing you
have to do. Betty says I am very bad at it, I say
so is Ambrosear. It is disgusting, Betty says
farght if you like, me. I didnt have to learn to
ride a donkey. I can ride a donkey in Greek.
Actuly the boy wipt me to make the donkey go,
it hurt more than the bounsing but it was
alright because I like donkeys. People like
difarent things I ough to like the horse, but
they ougth to like me, Fran and Robin, so I
know what the horse feels like. Actuly it is a
nice horse if you like that kind of thing. Now it
is out there eating up the downs, not like me I
cuoldnt eat, not any thing. I wuold rather have
a donkey from the donkey shop. So wuold they
if they knew. No, I am not thinking. They have
got me and thats to them a donkey but they
want a horse.

A donkey is afectonate,
   A horse is disdainful. Cant spell it.
A donkey is simpal,

A horse is complacted.
A donkey is cheep,
A horse is expansive.
A donkey is noisy,
A horse is hushful.
A donkey is ashamed of,
A horse is proud of,
A donkey is loveing.
There is a poem I think it is by Sir Jon
Bitumen about god going hey ho away we go
riding on a donkey. It was my joak or pugn,
and Fran agreed and Robin had to go for a
walk with his own legs to forget it. They dont
have poems about horses, only movies and
adavertesements of the bank. I have a red bead
purse, a red lether one, and a bright red vynil
one with a strap and not all that money.
Grandpa gets bags of money from the tills in
HEMPSTALL HEMPSTALL HEMPSTALL, Ive seen it they come
and get it in an armeured trolley and they wear
goggels to keep it from dazling them I think it
makes it inadvisable to them. I am only
writeing writeing writeing to stop from thinking
thinking thinking what they are doing and
what hapened. It has all hapened before and it
is all the same thing. I was little then, I thought
Fran was saving money up by not going to
work but actuly it was one of those ill times. I
thought she was all right now but it must of
got wurse or they wuold not of gone out. I

cannot ring any one, Christ was no good. Mrs
Fennal might be all right since she is mad
(~~uturely~~) (~~uttrely~~) quite and hasnt got a phone.
What I want is god on a donkey saying tabitha
cumi, beehold I have changed it from a horse
unto a donk and put the horse back with Betty
at Abots Lea. I didnt set eyes on Ambrosear
when I first saw it. It got named of a pudding I
think. Unless the pudding is tinned horse, but
actly the picture on the label is not of meat
but of sic in a bowl. I am being disrestpectful to
the maker but no one will read this.

Robin shook the rug out of the window, banged his head on
the frame, and dropped the rug.

'I wish you wouldn't help,' said Fran. 'Victoria, get up.'

Victoria got up, because she was being helpful too, in a way
that amused her. She had been lying in the place where the rug
should lie, and wanted Robin to drop it on her when he had
shaken it. Now it had gone down the side of the house.

'It's on the railings,' said Robin. 'I'll go for it.'

'The railing will be through it,' said Fran. 'I wish you wouldn't
bother with things you can't do. It doesn't matter in the least
what people think of the place. They must take us as they find
us. If it's a tip then that's the way we live. And it isn't anyone in
particular coming and not for long either.'

'Wendy,' said Victoria.

'That's why he's tidying up,' said Fran. 'Doesn't bother to
impress me any more: I can't do much for him. But Wendy,
that's a different thing.'

'I wish I'd got a stepmother,' said Victoria. She felt it was an interesting idea, and it had nothing to do with not wanting Fran. Fran understood what she meant.

'I must sound awful,' she said. 'I don't mean to. I'm sorry, Robin.'

'The input has been erased,' said Robin.

'And the output is on the railings,' said Fran.

Before going for the rug Robin came and gave her a hug and a kiss. Victoria joined in, and there was a squash of people for a time.

'Don't squeeze too hard,' said Fran. 'Wendy's a very unusual girl, so no wonder you find her fascinating.'

'Me?' said Robin. 'I have a bruise on the back of my head, and I am going down to pick up the rug. Is there anything you want from the car when I'm there?'

There was nothing wanted from the car. Today they were going to the farm, not for any reason that Victoria knew; a visit at the weekend, merely. But Robin could not drive so far, about eighty miles, and Fran was having one of her resting times when she was not very well, but not ill either. Wendy was coming up to Bristol to get her hair done, and she would take them to the farm, and probably bring them back the next day.

When she came she smelled very luxuriously of hairdresser's salon. She left the red Rover blocking up the end of the street, but the street was one that came to a stop at the gorge, so nothing would want to get far through.

'If you have to live in a town, this is the place to be,' said Wendy, looking from the window towards the gorge and the bridge. 'All this daylight. I must borrow some, and a mirror,

Fran, and patch up my surfaces. I expect I look as if I had come straight from the stage, putting on my face at the hairdresser's.'

Victoria went to watch the process. Fran had some powder and a tube of lipstick. She used the lipstick in cold weather when her lips cracked, and the powder when she had been cooking and thought she smelt of oven. But Wendy had a pack of stuff with her always. She said she had to keep her face in good repair, because that was all the world would see. She said her jaw was too big and too square, and her mouth not large enough.

'I'm a bit of a slab,' she said to Victoria. 'I've got to get dressed up. Now, your mother is beautiful, nice-shaped face, good complexion. She's right, she doesn't need anything. She's pale today, though. Fran,' she called, 'come through a minute, darling.'

Fran came through. 'A little treatment,' said Wendy. 'Just to brighten you up, a little pale, you are,' and she ran some pink powder round, and a touch of colour on the cheek. 'Look at you,' she said.

'I feel better,' said Fran.

'And me,' said Victoria, when Fran had got up. She sat in the chair.

'Dumplings have all the goodness inside,' said Wendy and gave her a red nose.

They were at the farm for lunch. They left their own bridge, and went over a huger longer one, nearly as high, nearly sea under it, not a trifling river. It was the Severn Bridge. Beyond was nearly Wales.

After lunch there was a walk.

The farm was mostly made of fields. Fields were much the

same to Victoria wherever she was. On the whole the Downs were better, though you could sometimes tread in things – 'Dogshot Park' Fran called the Downs on their dirty days: Robin knew that was irony but thought it might be a pun of some sort.

['Everywhere to get anywhere,' said Granny.]

There was to be no skulking by the fire, Grandpa said, looking at Fran, because he did not mean her. 'Come on, Queen,' he said to Victoria. 'Get some fresh air.'

Victoria did not want to walk anywhere. It had been fine in England, and now, in nearly Wales, it was drizzly; and the car radio forecast rain for Wales itself.

'Come on, Vict,' said Robin. 'Get the language off your face. God, now she's crying.'

'Come on, Elsie Dee,' said Fran.

'No,' said Robin, and he walked straight outside, thumping the door shut as he went, ashamed of Victoria, angered by her contrariness.

'Elsie who?' said Victoria. She longed to stay by the log fire: you can get air anywhere, but not log fire.

'L C D,' said Fran. 'Liquid Crystal Display. Tears.'

Grandpa put his arm round Fran. 'You don't need to come, sweetheart,' he said. 'No need to stir.'

Robin and Wendy, Fran and Grandpa, thought Victoria. Why don't they swap round? I'd stay by the fire. But, she thought, less clearly, this place is half Wendy, or half the place is Wendy, so a lot of it would be gone. 'I'll come part way,' said Fran. 'I'll be all right.'

'You'll want your glasses,' said Grandpa to Victoria.

She obediently got them, but did not intend to wear them for a few cold fields and their fat rain.

'You'll want to wave to your Welsh boys,' said Fran. 'Pop them in your pocket.'

'Welsh boys?' said Victoria, as stupidly as she could.

'Glasses,' said Fran. 'Bring your head as well. You'll need it.'

In fact Fran came with them all the way to the thing they had come for. Victoria was the one that did not know anything was in store. She walked along in a green world, better in some ways than Clifton Downs, the greenness uninterrupted, with no road, no smell of cars or houses, and with a feeling that it might be possible to go on for ever in the green, instead of arriving at Blackboy Hill or Redland.

'Now put your glasses on,' said Grandpa. 'You can't see without them. There now, what do you think?'

Victoria looked. She saw a field, with some woodland beyond it, a grey sky, the gate they were leaning on, and nothing else much. There was a lightish-coloured horse standing a bit in the way, obviously also finding nothing worth seeing. Because of it Victoria could not see all there was. She moved along the fence and looked round the creature, since Grandpa might not have taken it into account. There was more field and more woodland.

'What do you think?' called Grandpa. His voice lifted up with pleasure. 'She's yours, Queen, your very own.'

Victoria looked again. She, who, what, was hers? There was nothing; only the lightish horse. There was only this lightish horse.

Only this lightish horse.

She looked back at the group: Robin, Fran, Wendy, Grandpa,

all were looking at her; they were giving her something; was she giving them something?

There was only this lightish horse. There was probably a name for its colour. Pink. This pink horse.

She would love them for it, extra and especially and for ever. But she knew she would never love the horse. I am not turned on, she thought. Then the horse blistered and all the distant trees humped up, because the thing that squeezes tears out was squeezing now, the have-to-cry was crying her; and there was no one she could tell anything to; she had to be alone with the part of the gift she wanted: the giving of it from them all; and the part she did not want: the thing they had given.

Liquorice Crystal Allsorts, she thought, and tipped tears from the lenses of her glasses. Her nose began to run. 'Overcome, overwhelmed,' said Grandpa. 'Not a word to say, Queen?'

'It's alive,' she said.

'So it is,' said Grandpa. Then he was through the gate and bringing the horse to it. 'Name of Ambrosia,' he said. 'Not at all young, but a very steady mare, be like a mother to you. What do you think, shall we put you up on her now?' Victoria shook her head. 'Bit too much for you, eh? Well then, you lead her and she can be in the stable ready to go back with you tomorrow – better than being down here, always be handy for a ride.'

Victoria then hugged them all for their giving, and took the halter in her hand. There was a long time in the stable and in the tack room, talking about hay and leather, where the smells were too rich, before they got back by the fire again, where the smoke just hung on the air, and the smell of the polish on the furniture hung with it, and the great chairs were not like saddles but like howdahs, and the fire hissed and bubbled, and supper came hot on the trolley.

It was that sort of farm, where no one ate the pigs, just scratched their backs, and the same lambs were born each year to please, never chopped up; where calves the same colour had the same pet names, always young. But Victoria did not know it for years.

They went back in the Land Rover. The horse box was behind it. Victoria could remember not knowing what a horse box was, long after she had expected one with the rocking horse in. That time it had been the Transit.

The horse did not come quite home with them. They called at the end of the road to let Fran get off, and then went on across the bridge a mile or two further into fields again. Fran had given hard directions to Wendy, because Robin was no good at them.

They found a farm, down a lane. Here they were expected by a girl called Betty, who was to stable and look after Ambrosia and Victoria was to come here and ride. Betty was to give her lessons on riding.

The happening was different, as time went by. Part of a riding lesson is shovelling dirty straw before you begin, and the horse has to be brushed and combed as if it had hair all over its back and legs, not just on its tail and mane.

'Why, you can do ut, so you can,' said Betty. 'Get up on your toes, midear. Why, this be the sweetest little old mare I ever see, wouldn't tread on you, nor nothing, just an old sweetie, that's what she is. Now, let's have you up, well you are a lump, fat bum you got, but I won't call it a good seat. Now, straighten your back, hold with your knees, horse got to feel you somewhere.'

Victoria heard it all, knew it all, or recognized it when it came again. Even when she went hard at the work it was no good. She saddled Ambrosia herself, at last, and got up alone. Then Betty came up and gave her a little push and she toppled off the other side complete with saddle and stirrups and girth, and hung there with her hair in stable litter, while Betty laughed.

'And we thought it would be something for you to be doing,' said Robin, when Betty had at last telephoned to say the hay was finished, and what about another lesson for the little maid, ant seen she this long time?

'I had a lot of lessons,' said Victoria. 'I did a lot of lessons.'

'I wish this girl didn't telephone me,' said Robin. 'This is all your grandfather's business, not mine. He gave you the horse and he pays for everything. She should ring him.'

'Oh, come on,' said Fran. 'Victoria doesn't have to think about that. There's no real difficulty. You just tell Betty to order some hay or straw or whatever and when she gives you a bill you send it to your father. I don't see any problem.'

'It isn't a clear arrangement,' said Robin. 'Nobody says Father will want to pay for straw and oats or lessons, so I can't take it for granted.'

'It seems logical to me,' said Fran.

'That's just what it isn't,' said Robin.

Victoria hoped the subject might have been used up in the arguments about whether it made sense. It had not been.

'Now,' said Robin, 'I thought you'd been out there a lot more than five times.'

'Once we got lost,' said Victoria. 'Remember?'

'It wasn't just once you didn't get there,' said Robin.

Victoria had hoped the reality of that one time would overflow into all the others and obliterate them. At the time it had usefully taken a whole afternoon.

Robin had got her and the car over the bridge, but almost at once seemed to be in a different land, not in a road at all but in the drive of a large house, where there was nowhere to turn round. They had gone on and on, and come into the road again at an unknown place. Neither of them had had any idea where they were; none of the signposts said anything useful.

'This is a dilemma,' said Robin. 'All the roads go to unknown places; we wish to go to a known place, Clifton or Abbots Leigh; therefore we do not wish to go on any road; however, we have to keep moving or go nowhere and we must go on a road; so it is impossible for us to be saved; we are in a system that excludes our destination. I could work it out better if I did not have to do the steering.'

'I'll sing,' said Victoria. 'If it's going to be a long way back.'

It was a long way back, with help from a lot of people, and a great deal of driving through Bristol, at which Robin was very inefficient, not only about going on the right road, but about going along the right side of it and seeing traffic signals. He would stop at a red light saying CHEMIST, and always had to be hooted at to move off on the green.

'I got lost once,' said Robin. 'It won't account for them all.'

'No theory is complete,' said Victoria. It must be right, because Robin had said it more than once.

'I'll take her on Saturday,' said Fran. 'I'll settle about the hay and anything else, because I don't feel anything strange about your father wanting his granddaughter to have hay and stabling for her horse, and paying for it. I'm not shy about it. So I'll go, and meanwhile I'll sort out with madam here about those missing lessons. How many lessons has Christabelle Llewellyn had instead of you Vict?'

'Christ?' said Victoria. 'None.' Christabelle had never been told about the pink horse.

'I wish you wouldn't call her that,' said Robin.

'Yes,' said Fran. 'Christ. Your friend.'

'I just do Social Service with her,' said Victoria. 'Mrs Fennal. We both do Mrs Fennal. We do Mrs Fennal together.'

'Ah,' said Fran, 'your Mrs Fennal.'

'You think they're imaginary,' said Victoria. 'Don't you? Christ and Mrs Fennal.'

'There is something imaginary,' said Fran. 'What's been going on?'

'Nothing, nothing, nothing,' said Victoria. But Fran pursued her argument. It was true that nothing had been going on about riding lessons, but that kind of truth is not the whole of the matter. Fran pinned it all down, finding that Victoria had led a real life of crime by going to the same Christabelle's house once for the afternoon; by going with the aforesaid (some swearing? Victoria wondered, not knowing the word) Christabelle too far on the bus twice, once to Nailsea and finding nothing to do there, and once to Clevedon and not doing much better; by going nowhere twice, wandering down into Clifton and looking in shops and spending the bus fare on an orange drink, like two old ladies taking tea.

When Fran had found it all out she was not having it any more. Victoria knew she had been bound to find out. She thought, as she was scolded, that Fran had to come to one of two conclusions: that she did not want to learn to ride and have a horse, or that she should be punished by having it taken away. Either would do.

But Fran was too kind for that. She was content to be angry. She telephoned Betty and talked to her, and found out that Victoria was not a very promising rider and might have felt discouraged at her lack of progress, 'not having no notion of a canter, not yet, but she might do it, hopefully,' Betty said.

On Saturday Fran took her to Abbots Leigh, and sat in the car while Victoria went through her slow paces.

'You want to ride yourself, Mrs Hemst,' said Betty.

'One day,' said Fran. 'But not just now.'

The Saturday after that Victoria was totally embarrassed, because a pony club was meeting at Betty's yard. She sat on Ambrosia, a pinky light colour, not wanting to be up there, surrounded by expert little girls on little ponies that they loved. They even loved each others' ponies in a spiteful way. Victoria felt like an idiot, an angry idiot. She only had to say out loud that she did not want or like having a horse, even Ambrosia with her gentle personality. But she would rather hurt herself than tell so many people that they had made the wrong choice for her, and ask whether she could trade for a donkey.

The next Saturday again was cold. Halfway through the lesson ('lift up your bum, sit upright, you still en't got it,') Fran came into the yard from where she had been waiting.

'We've got to go,' she said. 'Thank you Betty; I've got a bad pain coming on, we'd better go home at once.'

'You do look rough, Mrs Hemst,' said Betty.

'Ring my husband,' said Fran. 'Vict, get in the car.'

'Is it all right?' said Victoria.

'Jump in,' said Fran. 'It isn't quite as it should be. I wouldn't have come out this afternoon if I could trust you.'

They drove off. They had to stop just before the bridge while Fran had an acute spasm. Victoria sat beside her in a different kind of pain. But before Victoria's pain had become too much to bear, Fran's was better too. She started the car again and drove on.

Robin was waiting at the end of the road. 'I'll park the car,' said Fran. 'Turn it round for you. Go in and call an ambulance. I'll stay here. I'm not going to walk all the way up the stairs just to come down again.'

Victoria was not there in what followed, except that she was often in the way and had to be moved aside.

The ambulance came ringing up the hill, and then backed into the road. Fran got out of the Renault, walked into the ambulance by herself, and lay on a stretcher.

'I'll be all right,' she said. 'Robin, ring Wendy and ask her to come down for a few days. Vict, be helpful. Robin, you ring the hospital and see when you can come to visit me.'

Then the doors were closed on her, and off she went.

Wendy was at the house before dark. 'I came at once,' she said. 'Put the kettle on. What does the hospital say?'

There was nothing said that night. In the morning the telephone rang. Robin was upon it before it got into full voice. 'It's for you,' he said, giving it to Victoria.

Betty was speaking. 'How bist thee? Just wondering how your mum be,' she said. 'I never realized her was in that condition, never give it a thought.'

'Condition?' said Victoria.

'In foal,' said Betty. 'Has she dropped it yet?'

'I don't know what you mean,' said Victoria.

'Is it born?' the telephone wanted to know, ridden by Betty.

Victoria said nothing. Of course it would be alive, but living? That was different.

'Boy or a girl, man or woman, colt or filly?' said Betty.

'I don't know,' said Victoria. She turned to ask Wendy. 'Is it a boy or a girl?'

'Don't know yet,' said Wendy. Victoria told Betty.

'I always say, it dun't really matter,' said Betty. 'Don't thee forget to tell I.'

Wendy put an arm round Victoria. 'We don't think it's going to be anything,' she said. 'It's much too soon. There's something a bit wrong, but hospitals know all about that.'

Things went on being wrong. Victoria lived in two levels at a time. She was unable to separate her mind from what was going on in an unknown hospital, so that her days at school were thinly lived out above reality, and she was both present and absent. At home the essence of the place had dried up. Wendy stayed most of the time, but had to go back on two nights. When she was there she was not the full Wendy of the farm, and when she was not there nothing was. Robin sat in his chair disconnected too, with little to say, one ear towards the telephone.

'It's a fight,' he said. 'It's all or nothing, on or off.'

'We'll see,' Wendy said. And she cooked them a different set of meals from the ones they were used to. They were right for the farm, but wrong for the flat.

The next Saturday Wendy went to see Fran in the morning and Robin went in the afternoon. Wendy took Victoria out to Abbots Leigh.

'Why, 'tes Miss Evans,' said Betty. 'You Victorial's auntie, then?'

'Step grandmother,' said Victoria.

'I never,' said Betty. 'Well.' She shook her head, not seeing Miss Evans as belonging to anyone at all.

'Mrs Hempstall is still in hospital,' said Wendy, unable to explain how she was not quite a lady. 'She's still very poorly, and we don't know what to expect, so there isn't any news.'

Then she solved the problem Victoria was facing, showing how bad she was at riding, by going off into Nailsea to see an old friend for an hour.

'Now there's a horseman,' said Betty.

But Victoria sat down on a heap of dung and cried and cried, and told Betty plainly about everything, about not being a very pleasing person, about Fran frightening her too much this last week, about not wanting to ride on anything more than a seaside donkey, about not being able to spell or tell the truth, and it was never going to be possible to canter. And she would rather have told Wendy whom she adored.

'Well, there now,' said Betty, and got her a clean, spotted handkerchief. 'We can't tell what's in a mind, can us? But 'tes best spat out and got rid. I tell 'ee, have one of my humbugs,' and she brought out a paper bag with them in, 'and the old mare will have one too, there,' Brosial, you do like that; she do like they marvellous. Now just hop up with 'ee and see about that canter, then 'tis done. And Miss Evans would like to see that, wouldn't her?'

When Wendy came back Victoria was cantering, two bounces out of three.

'Coming along,' said Wendy.

When they got home Robin was upset but not tense. 'She's all right,' he said. 'At last.'

'Anything else?' said Wendy.

'There won't be anything else,' said Robin.

They've just got me still, Victoria thought. But after this afternoon's talk to Betty she felt that she was glad of that, even if no one else was. I'm not what they want, but I'm what I've got. I have to live with me too.

Eleven

DIARY I am dareing to remeber. It was not a very good baby I heard them say another time. Robin was anxieux, his eyes were trangulier like the wurrid dog in the lady and the tramp. I hate hearing that about the baby, it isnt meant 4 my intalect 2 know. Actuly it is all strange now. I am quite near the horse. If I take off my glasses it is like a sunset, pinkish, its colour. I have come outside. I have evoided Mr Pattypatty down the stairs, and bruogt my computor paper and two pens. I am where I left the horse, which is where it is. It is all very quiet. The shops are closed I dont know why, the pubs are open. I am by the george, there is the bridge I have broken the rules of. I dont know anyone in the world. Even Paul the boy cant be here, I saw him at Abots Lea, gowing. It is better here, the house was getting smaller and so was i. i wish (†) i knew sombody. (†) I cuold not take the horse back even if it is free on the bridge, after I broke the law. They know a pink horse called Ambroseal by Bolians. Actuly I am quite used to the horse and it understands me. I wish I knew some one. I keep writeing wishes more than three times. But I never get them even one time. I have never cried in public since, or not when any public was there. I mean this is a public place but actuly I am only putting my head on my clean knees. I remeber going down the (sligh) (glide) on the wrocks over there, a lot of people were sliding. I slided on to the concrete and Robin wuoldnt even look at the place. I was children then, children cry. Children are not a good idea(l). I dont know which is the right word, like a Bolian. I ougth to take the things off the horse but I can not do any thing, I am only just my glasses and my knees and my fingers. Between is the runes of my (brian) brain.

I need my system cleaned of old programs and garbage I ougth to go on stand-by. Robin says they get the (equivi) (equalav) like nigthmares, bad computor dreames. Computurs shuold try actul living awake somtime, a nigthmare wuold be pieceful I cuold go on sitting here for ever, no one wuold know, I have got outside every thing. Every thing I am doing dosnt afect me, it dosnt afect any one. What are Robin and Fran doing? It must be worse. In a minuet I will go and look at the house. They have not sent for Wendy, if they did it wuold be three red cars. Perhaps it is too late. Some body come. Christ says she has a boy but I think she

*is only saying it. I have a Xtmas card, and he
has been near me. The day after tomorrow it will
be six months ago, because of 23rd of June now.*

Paul had been near. But he did not know whether he was being rejected or ignored. Were they deciding not to write to him? Were they busy with other things? Was there some other person in his place?

'Wake out of it,' said Angela, in the new year. 'Has she gone with your wits?'

'I don't know,' said Paul. 'Is this sort of thing common; does it often happen?'

'I couldn't say,' said Angela. 'If you let it I suppose it might. Why don't you go and see her?'

'Invite her to tea,' said Mum. Angela, of course, promoted this sort of conversation in front of the whole family at any time.

'I don't know where she lives,' said Paul.

'Look in the telephone book,' said Angela. 'To begin with. You don't know anything and everything.'

And Mum smiled, as knowing as Angela, unlikely as that must be. How could Mum have been here?

There the desired name was, clearly printed, R.C. Hempstall, and the address that it must be, trailing after the numbers of the different departments, stores, and warehouses of HEMPSTALL MARKETING at Keynsham, Oldland Common, Old Market, Shirehampton, Stokes Croft, Brislington, Whitchurch, intervening civil neighbourhoods.

He knew the road. He had been along it. The old houses

faced the gorge and looked at the bridge. He went along it again. In one of these cars she sat and breathed; the air on the street itself had been moved about by her. That did not mean much, he thought: all the air he breathed and moved about had already been breathed by dinosaurs, moved by iguanodon. Iguanodon climbs up out of the gorge, threatens Wendy Victoria Hempstall, from number 30 in this road. Paul Creasey in the far corner defending her, by a heroic act of leverage casts the amazing swamp beast down into its filthy lair, shattering every bone in its body, and the lovely maiden is . . . still invisible, locked away in the house of her choice, not calling for rescue, not noticing him. Iguanodon slumbers.

He saw her several times. What do you say to them? Angela could not know; nothing had knocked at her heart. Once, even unexpectedly, not thinking of her at the time, he had rubbed shoulders with her when she came out of a shop doorway. He had smiled a stuck smile that would not go away, that turned into a fixed grin, and then, he knew, into an appalling set grimace that hurt him.

'I'm glad to see you,' he said.

'How do you do?' she said. 'Have you seen my mother?'

'No,' said Paul.

'I expect she'll find me,' said Victoria. 'I haven't got my glasses on, so I can't see across the road.'

'Would you like a cup of coffee,' said Paul. It was a remark, not a question in a formal sense.

But the moment had gone. Her mother came and Victoria went away before she formed another word. He saw her looking about for him and being unable to distinguish him from the blur round her, and that was it. He could not follow.

Instead he went up on the bridge and traced out among the houses hanging at the edge of the gorge the one that must be hers, and wondered which might be her window.

Then boldly, some day in spring, on a Saturday morning, he walked to the street, to the house, to the door, put his hand to the bell. Then took it away and turned his back on it, walked back down the street and out of it. He walked about the roads there for an hour, cursing his weak shyness, knowing he had lost the only opportunity there would be.

He stood on a corner and gathered himself again. He put the order of things in his mind, and set out on the program again. Along the street, to the door, a hand to the bell. A finger that would not touch. He defied the coward finger. He leaned forward and the finger had to press the button. The bell sounded within the house.

A man came to the door. 'Whom did you want?' he asked.

'Miss Hempstall,' said Paul.

'Top flat,' said the man. 'Go on up.'

'Thank you,' said Paul.

'Lot of people don't know,' said the man. 'Right to the top.'

Paul went right up to the top. He was fairly sure he had got to it, but there was the shape of another flight going higher. He had not thought of a flat, only of a whole house belonging to the Hempstalls.

While he stood for a moment he realized that he was hearing a quarrel from the other side of the door. There was an argument going on. He decided that the morning had failed him. He had not struck the first time, and had missed his opportunity. He looked at the bland door that barred his way, the door he did not want to have opened now, and turning from it, went downstairs, and out of the house, away.

That afternoon he was driven to try again. This time he walked into the house and went up the stairs to the door. There was only the murmur of music beyond it now. He tapped on the broad white surface.

There was time to run, and no time to run. The door opened. A man holding a bundle of computer paper and with a slightly Afro hairstyle and a moustache said, 'Yes?' his mind still on the papers.

'Miss Hempstall,' said Paul. Not a question, again, merely a search for her reality, her existence.

'Out riding,' said the man. 'Any messages?'

'Oh, no thanks,' said Paul, now that she existed in another mind, even if not in a related continuum. 'Another time.'

And he went away, wondering whether there would be another time, conscious of the finality of her not being there at that eternal moment, himself trembling and blushing by the railings, the shouts of strange Clifton children swarming the streets round him, alien as love.

Twelve

DIARY If we hadnt had the longest day (21st)
this wuold be it (23rd), and I have been writing
it for years. It is problby the end of the world as
well, I know the feeling, all the shops are shut,
a sure sighn of things. But nothing is hapening,
I wuold not mind if it did. The grass is dry as
hair and the same colour but there are aunts in
it, also a centrepede which went out of sight
before it got too far away to see. But that is not
reallyality. Low forms will survive the holly
course at the end of the world Robin says. They
are more logical he says, they can not have
dilemma. But Robin is not going to be at the
end of the world.

I do not actuly think it is today. I do not
think it is actuly now. I think Fr ——— I think
somthing has hapened to our famaly. I am
sitting here not writeing it down. I am gowing
round and round the garden like a teddy baer
at it. Actuly I am frigthened. Robin says it is
ilogical to be frigthened, it is the effect of a
series of impressions before they are sorted. But
he has not been there, like the end of the world.

Praps I am the end of the world too. I am seeping out of my senses. I am the boy that is alive at the end of the world with just his horse but the boy likes that, and I dont. He jumps over the george on the horse, like a miricale or vision, on a black man horse not a pink lady horse. I am convinsed of that. It is no better waiting here than waiting in the house. Coming out was like leaving after the stable door.

I have got up and actuly caught the horse, they get quite dosile when not alarming, not to jump the george, I just need sombody. I got hold of the rains and it shook its head up and down greatly but not often and that was all its act, it is now eating grass. There are people on the bridge and I can hear music but I do not know why unless sombody has a tranny in the wrocks.

I could ride down to Christs, but am not sure of stopping at lights ect ect on the way all so, it is obvious to walk across roundabouts but problby ilegall. If I had (curage) (corauge) cuorage I wuold ride to the farm, but where is it and is it very far by horse?

I cuold of gone today to Mrs Fennal with Christ. It is all right with her, she is mad the same all ways. Robin says insain is as good as sain, but it can not be or he wuold not go insain at (knocky knocky) gnocchi gnocchi whose there. I have reached a salution, I am an

112

ugly duck that grew from an ugly duckling.

The duck lived on Mrs Fennal's bed. The school Social Service had befriended Victoria and Christabelle Llewellyn to her, and prescribed a charitable visit each week. It happened from the third form up, beginning with easy visiting to old people who were merely lonely or slightly handicapped, and going on in higher forms to those with problems of harder sorts like eleven delinquent babies and a hard-core passion for bingo.

'Talk to the people you are taking over from,' said the organizer at school. 'Find out about your person. In this form your person is an old person and will have got used to last year's helpers. So be considerate. Last year's helpers will go with you the first time and introduce you. If you have any problems at all come straight to me.'

'You won't have any problems,' said Victoria's and Christabelle's two fourth-formers. 'She's got a bad leg but a brilliant memory. You'll find she's taking care of you, not you of her. But don't take any notice of what she says. She's got these old-fashioned political ideas. We liked her, but this year we've got a young mother and her baby.' They longed for the baby because he was a boy and they would bath him, they were sure.

'Yuk,' said Christabelle. Victoria said nothing. She had no opinion at all about babies, not wanting to think about them.

Mrs Fennal was used to herself, and the fourth-formers were used to her as well. Victoria, who had to have things pointed out to her before she saw them and formed opinions, found nothing odd for a time. Christabelle, who saw everything and had opinions before fact and thought about nothing, was soon shocked.

Mrs Fennal had a dark ground-floor flat. The darkness was her own doing. She had filled the windowsills inside and out with pots and troughs ('trows', she called them) with plants growing in them. Outside the windows, on the ground, she had tubs with trees growing. One was so tall that the man upstairs had to take his shears to it and clip the top level to stop it covering his window.

'I have 'em like that so I don't need to go out to water them in wet weather,' said Mrs Fennal. 'I got the rising damp in one leg already; don't want it any higher in my vital parts.'

'You wouldn't need to water them on wet days,' said Victoria. 'Would you?'

'Damn government we get now there ent no proper wet days,' said Mrs Fennal. 'I used to be on the side of the government, but not any longer. It hasn't moved with the time, that be why.'

Mrs Fennal was eighty-seven years old. She knew what she was saying and whether it was firm truth or jest or harmful lie. She was mad, perhaps, but not out of her everyday senses: she knew what caused weather and what caused governments. She put her large head on one side and looked at the girls.

'That's what my father says,' said Victoria, leaving aside the question of rain. Robin had no good opinion of how anyone ran anything. Mrs Fennal went on looking with cocked head. 'But not about the weather,' said Victoria at last, forced to speak.

'We don't believe that,' said Christabelle Llewellyn. 'About the weather. You've been reading science fiction.'

'Hook me,' said Mrs Fennal. 'You can hit a capitalist government with anything. 'Tis no way to run the country. And now the queen, a very fine lady, no doubt, but what be that to do with we working folk?'

'It's a very good thing to have a queen,' said Christabelle firmly. 'And a government. It depends which side got in.'

'Don't have more than one side and you got no problems,' said Mrs Fennal. 'Ha. Hook me, hang the lot, I say.'

'That would be wicked,' said Christabelle. 'I don't think you should talk like that.'

'I ent bloodthursday,' said Mrs Fennal. 'I'd give they a warning. Nobody ent obliged to be in government. Then I'd have the revolution, and I've got my red flags to hang out I ent afraid.'

Mrs Fennal had plenty of red flags. She had them hung on her walls, along with Chinese and Russian posters that were probably about revolutions. The girls, washing up for her, used red cloths. Then they washed the cloths out.

'The dye runs,' said Christabelle.

'Blood,' said Mrs Fennal. 'Hook me, so it be.'

She was not into active revolution any more because of not going out of the flat and its tiny triangle of garden. 'There ent even hardly any plans in the house, not like one time, when us had some real live ones. Dictectives used to come and see I, questions about the revolution, what it did be. But all my lively rascals did die and come to nought. The dictectives never got nothen neither.'

Christabelle was of the opinion that the dead had choice of heaven afterwards.

'Damn rubbish that, hook me,' said Mrs Fennal. 'That be just the travel agents saying that so to keep in a job. No, you got to have a revolution today and get heaven now.'

Mrs Fennal, prepared to hang all members of the government after a warning, was unable to stop herself helping any plant or animal that seemed homeless or unwanted. Even eating was for her an act of cruelty to a cabbage or underprivileged ear of wheat or bereaved hen.

'But if I don't eat,' she said, ''tis cruel to I.'

'About the only thing you can eat is pebbles and fallen apples,' said Christabelle. She was convinced that Mrs Fennal was being cruel to the duck when she asked them to bring some small gritty stones for it, as if it fed only on them. It changed her attitude towards the duck. Victoria had always been ready to accept it, and the way it slept on Mrs Fennal's bed – it seemed to her that Mrs Fennal was old enough to have a live creature, while Victoria herself when she was a small child, had had to have toy ones, a lizard called T Rex.

Mrs Fennal's duck was called Mandy. She said it had been shot by a capitalist wide-boy proprietor. It had lost part of a wing, one foot, and an eye. It was a very ugly duck by now. It would rap you on the ankle as you walked past.

'Don't 'ee fret none,' said Mrs Fennal when Christabelle was inclined to be indignant and feel hurt about it. 'A duck ent got teeth no more. Ducks do have grinders.' Christabelle was never clear about what the gritty pebbles were for.

She had a hard time accepting the use the bath was put to.

The duck swam about in it. In cold weather the water was warmed. Victoria did not know much about cleaning a bath, and did not like it any more or any less after the duck had been in it. Christabelle was ready to oblige, as a novelty, but not after the duck.

'My mother says they usually keep coal in the bath,' she said. 'Not animals. We get spiders in ours, in the week. My dad gets them out Saturdays. He's a fan, we're not.'

However, Christabelle was ready to tackle Mrs Fennal on the subject, and tell her she should use the bath herself.

Mrs Fennal looked at her, head on one side. 'You come bath night and lift I out,' she said. 'I can't manage to be in and out of that tub. What you're saying is class prejudice. But how often do you get a wash all over?'

'Every Saturday,' said Christabelle. 'Sometimes on Wednesday as well. We have to take a shower at school.'

'I get a wash all over every day,' said Mrs Fennal. 'Best I can, hobbling about like I do. Comrades in revolution got to keep clean. Who knows, we might all be living together, and we don't aim for no stinking revolution.'

Round Easter there began to be a strong musty smell in the flat. One day, when the girls were there, Mrs Fennal was having a shouting contest with the old man upstairs. The shouting was about something she had done and shouldn't have, or shouldn't have done, and had. She didn't ought to have had them, said the old man, and she did ought to have kept them. So it was a riddle.

Mrs Fennal was cross and would not say what it was about, but the old man was a capitalist lackey and running jackal, and on the day she would be up there, bad leg or not, and finish him. 'Junival,' she said. 'Sixty-six years old, knows the lot. Hook me, don't know nothen at that age.'

And somebody had eaten all her food, and the duck's. 'Maybe inflation done it,' she said, putting her head to one side.

It was mice. Mrs Fennal had a problem, in taking the first pair of mice, letting them live in a cupboard and breed there, very tame as they were, and then finding they had over-run the flat. The problem had gone upstairs too and was eating her food. She could not bring herself to trap the mice or have them trapped. The matter was dealt with by the council, who sent a man round. The two girls were left to pick up 107 bodies from the cupboards and shelves and garden. Mrs Fennal could not see all these little mortalities, or their mass grave in the dustbin.

One day, limping more than usual, she explained about her leg. 'I wasn't very clear about the revolution then,' she said. 'Once the Irish got away, when I was a grown girl and working in Wales. Revolution, they had. Then they had it in Russia the next year. Then a few years later we thought we'd have one. Trouble was, there wasn't enough in Wales wanted it, so we had to make do with just a few, and I got blowed up with dynamite. They caught I, and did put I in prison. Locked up, I was, like a criminal.'

That had been nearly seventy years ago. Now they were not allowed to hold it against her, and she did not have to speak about it, but she was proud of it, and was ready to go to prison again, if the revolution came.

Victoria thought it was an interesting fact. Robin would

have said there was no reason to have an opinion about the matter; it was merely information. But Christabelle was horrified. When she heard it she went away at once, and took the message home, and her mother took it on to the Social Service organizer at school.

Robin was not worried. 'There's worse things than crypto-communists,' he said to Victoria. 'I think Fran is a crypto-Liberal.'

Christabelle and her mother came slowly round to understanding that Mrs Fennal's prison sentence did not matter any more. 'It actually happened before my grandfather was born,' said Christabelle. 'Mrs Fennal was a political prisoner, like the Russians.'

However, when Christabelle went back to Mrs Fennal and explained that point to her she had a sound scolding for sympathising with enemies of the perfect state, and had to sob a little because Mrs Fennal convinced her about some thing, though she did not know what. Victoria thought Christabelle was being driven into a corner by meeting someone with decided opinions. Victoria was used to Robin and knew how to walk round decided opinions that had nothing to do with her own thoughts.

To cheer Christabelle, Mrs Fennal undid a fat roll of paper and exposed plans and drawings of the Suspension Bridge.

'Made from the originals,' she said. 'This be what we worked out seventy year since. I got charge of the plot. See these red numbers. Well, those be where we do put the dynamite when the time do come. Where we put it and blow the bridge, and down it come and block the river. There be Bristol out of the action, and there I be with a red flag holding Clifton. You come round that day, and I'll enrol you.'

'Oh,' said Christabelle, understanding how to act. 'I shan't say a word.'

'That's my good little maid,' said Mrs Fennal. 'You'm bound to see social sense at last; you come here on Social Service after all.'

'I don't think I'll tell my mum,' said Christabelle, outside the house again. 'It wouldn't come right if I did.'

Thirteen

DIARY For a boy at the end of the world left
with his horse it would be a bond between them
like tarson and the (~~monky~~) monkey, a strange
affect I read about. Robin says it is an atribeaut
of simpal minds to think directaly and logicaly
but remeber that the simpalisaty of ignorance is
different than the simpalisaty of elegance. Well I
dont know which is between me and
Ambrosear, but in actul fact it came near and
got itself caught and nodded its head and I
looked up and saw the RENNOW, visable
between the beatle and the mg. I had to clean
my glasses on my shirt. I am going to look
unsteupid and to do my best. They have been a
long time coming back. Praps Robin was
driveing. I am going thruogh my intalect and
getting it in order, it is fine I am carm. Nothing
has hapened exept in the runes of my brain.

DIARY Now I am back sitting in the same
place, as if I didnt move at all. I still do not
know anything. I got on the horse. We went
round the camera(l) obscura(l). I think Betty
must of taught it well if I can do it better than

Robin drives a car. I went continuedly on down the road, I never did that before in town, and in our road, lo and beehold the Rennow had gone again. If it was there I could tell who drove, Fran goes too far and comes back into the space, Robin goes in frontly and crookid. But it wasnt there, so a mystrey. I parked the horse like a motor bike tide to the railings. I thuoght they wuold of been in, but only the ghost of them active with the toilet sistine filling, Robin used it last the seat was up. On the kitchen table Robin left a note, VICT written on it. I put it in my pocket and I came out. No one cuold of told I was there, exept I took the note, if you knew there was a note. Exept from one thing which the horse left, a big— I am not going to write it down to be seen, but say the word then read the note. A great big—.

A succession of still mist-ridden days hung with Paul for the rest of his life. They were the days and times and flavour of the late winter of that year. Such times and days and such weather had been before, but they had not been associated with a person. Now they were linked with, and seemed part of, Wendy or Victoria, the enchanted road, the magic house.

He wondered what he would have felt in a different winter. In deep snow and tearing winds would he have carried with him a harder picture of the girl? Since he saw more of the weather than he saw of her, and had to gain his impressions somewhere other than from her, he derived them mostly from the mild winter with its hanging sun and veiling mists, its warmth and placidity.

It was pleasure to walk the streets as he did in the lengthening evenings and on Saturdays and Sundays. It was some time before Angela told him to look in the telephone book for the address. Before he did that he had a false finding of her.

By chance, one Saturday morning, when he had been taking a pair of shoes to be mended at a shop where Mum thought they did it better than anywhere else, and he had volunteered to take them because the shop was in Clifton, not in Redland, and the mile and a half over the Downs was delight to him to walk, he saw her with another girl. The pair of them had been shopping and had a basket and a paper bag. Paul was the other side of the street, and stopped to look. Somebody walked into him because he had stopped in the way.

He was glad to be distracted, because he did not know what to do. Other people, in other scenes and under other skies, would cross the road and mind would speak to mind. Then he reflected that he knew those workings only from film and story, not from any acts of life. The instruction books were wrong; they were not like Dad's detailed drawings and notes about the ride, measured to make, constructed to fit, assembling into something.

The ride was indeed a toy of a small part of being and so were the glossy drawings on television screens and on the pages of books. But they pretended that all life was a toy; he did not want the toy life; he wanted instructions on reality and its faults. Nothing tells me, myself, he thought, how to cross the road. Nothing tells me how to match the pace of her heart to the pace of mine. Nothing indicates how she should ride my ride, or I should ride hers.

I don't want to get it wrong; but doing nothing is automatically wrong.

He saw them go in at the door of a council flat. He knew what that meant. Angela had her own fierce dirty twins to see at times. No one at home wanted to know about them, Mum pointing out that they had their own problem of Tiny Wee to clear up after. So Paul was now seeing the school Social Service working, and it was quite clearly something he could not be part of. It was not a time to approach.

It was not a time for waiting, either, to see Wendy's way home after she finished. The idea stood over him that it would be unlucky to stay where he was. Besides, he had not yet delivered the shoes.

He left the trail to go cold on that day. He half wondered whether she would write to him: she had his name and address. But the best he hoped from that was a card next Christmas, and that would not be fair, since Dad and Mum had decided to send no more cards at Christmas at all, or at least not for a few years. It had been half a resolution, and the other half consisted of writing more frequently to relatives who had had only Christmas cards lately.

Then the prospect of finding became less important than the looking. Searching itself occupied his thought. How to look was something he knew but had not yet done; finding, and what to do when he had found, were things he knew nothing about.

Finding was what he was setting out to do and was not

ready to do. I shall not die, he thought, like the poet; and of course the poet had not died, but sat down to write about it afterwards. I am the solid sort and I shall not even do that.

He spent some weeks in a happy misery. The day breaks not, he remembered from somewhere, it is my heart. Why is there something that takes my breath away? As I come round a corner into a street where she might be, and she is not there, why does my breath expand in my body? It is not seeing her, since she was not there.

Some countries, never your own, again, have a system of introduction; fathers go out and buy them; or the other father sells them, for so many cows: I know nothing about cows, only a little about wooden horses.

'It's love,' said Angela. 'We get a lot of it at school. It's obviously the same for boys as it is for girls. Though of course nothing like that happens to me, I'm glad to say.'

'Nothing wrong with what do happen to he,' said Dad.

Paul said nothing. But it was happening to him, as Dad said, and they seemed to have forgotten what it really was, or never to have known. Has each of us, or am I alone, a private heart?

He wandered the steep paths of the gorge on drizzling afternoons, wondering whether he would strike on some new view of where she lived, or upon her herself. Would she lean against some garden wall, hung on the rock, and be waiting for him? Would he, by finding her, pierce to the centre of the ache he felt, the pain that came from knowing she existed and could not be found? He felt that the pain would be with him always, the aching for ever, no more to be forgotten than the sea.

And there were times when he knew the search was over. Once in a street of Clifton he drew alongside her, suddenly unafraid of the meeting, and looked at her face, only to have been misled by her hair and back view: this was some other girl, with a squat nose, wide mouth, and, his memory told him later, tusks like a boar.

Another time as he went down the steep corkscrew, upriver of the Suspension Bridge, towards the Hotwells, he knew she was running down after him, and waited for her as she came laughing with a friend. But it was two dark romping detestable strangers. Who, worst of all, looked and looked at him before giggling on their way, swinging their bottoms from side to side, flaunting, despising.

Whenever he came to all the places where she was not, she filled that space pre-emptively. It was like hearing the echo of a sound, coming too late to hear the sound itself. Often he wished for holiday from her, who was to him alone his sun.

The next time he saw her, he thought, he would feel nothing. After all, there are things I do not like, one in particular.

The riding had hurt him at first. He had known Angela's friends, and he had heard of children round him as he grew up. But for them ponies happened in books and in them to a secret society of superior children. How could Victoria be so strange, so set aside, so much belong to a part of existence so imaginary? And of course, be at the same time a disobedient schoolgirl, scolded by Angela?

He saw her on the horse one day as they went to Nailsea. Tiny Wee saw the pink horse first.

'That's her, Paul,' said Angela. 'Getting a lesson.'

She was with Betty, about to cross the road. Betty was on a dark brown horse.

'Looks a bit rough for her mother,' said Angela. 'Our mothers don't look like that.'

'Yours does,' said Mum. 'Just another local girl.'

'That's the ideal,' said Angela. She looked hard at Paul, and he knew she was joking about the Bristol 'l' at the expense of Mum, who did not know there was a joke going on. His own family was taking itself to pieces. But he was helping, because he knew about that speech habit, though not always when he was using it; Mum did not ever know. Unfair he thought. Unfair: Angela is not using any kinds of love.

But Mum did know, and was hurt. 'I've said something stupid,' she said. 'Don't tell me; I don't want to know. But you wouldn't know if we hadn't sent you to find out. So don't mock.'

Now even the road to Nailsea was haunted. Both sides of the gorge were lands of dream. Only Redland, which was home, and school, were free. Now, when they went down to the barn and worked on the ride he felt he might be come upon by her and her real horse, among all his artificial ones, and that she would despise their wood and paint, as representing a false notion of how things were done.

But he knew that what he and Dad were working on was equally real, so he would not be able to admit what Victoria said, if she said it. He hated the notion, the idea, the ideal, of the pink horse, and was despondent at the thought of her riding it.

In the middle of the year, coming back with Dad in Tina, drawing the last trailer, full of spare parts and tools, he saw the pink horse on the edge of the Downs beside the Camera Obscura (he had gone one day to look at the words and see how they ended, so that he said them right). There was a saddle on it, but no rider. As soon as he could he hurried back to the place.

He had known, as he came, that the horse would be gone. He thought it, Victoria herself, might have had to wait until the bridge was open, because today was Midsummer, and the Midsomer Fayre parade had crossed, the bridge closed to ordinary traffic. The horse indeed had gone. He had time for a short cast round to see whether it might be at another likely place.

He ran down the hill towards her house. He did not see her. He went into the road, and she was not there, and neither was the horse.

But it had been there. In the middle of the road there was a neat heap of warm reeking horse dung, freshly down. That was the only signal.

He went up the hill again. He was wanted a mile away, so he hurried. It had been pointless to come, he thought. All he had got was hot. He felt he too must steam, newly fallen.

The horse was by the Camera Obscura again, close by the end of the bridge. Victoria was sitting on the ground, writing or drawing. He walked over to her. Now was the very time he did not want to see her, when he could not stay or stand.

It was writing she was engaged in. She wrote deliberately, placed a full stop, lifted her head, clicked the pen cap down with her thumb and said, firmly, without addressing Paul in particular, 'Shit.'

Fourteen

DIARY A word is a word. Robin says so, its his
rules. It dosnt remind you of anything else, he
says. Fran says he must wrong or he wuoldnt
make such a fuss about it. We had this actul
thing, and Fran said she will not listen to that
word, and all computors dont talk the same
language and she dosnt either. It wuold be
simpaler she said to train the horse, after all we
trained Vict (they did'nt, I develoded). Then she
was (on about) saying logicaly about Dogshot
Park, and Robin gets driven insain with that,
and Fran said Go to Haricot, and Robin said
Dont drop the standard of intalect. That might
be another pugn.

I am writeing this so I dont look up becaus
the boy is there an inch 25 gillimetres away, a
funny feeling, I said the horse word at his face,
he was just there. I mind what he thinks,
perhaps he is the only person I have seen for a
long time, I mean spoken to, and then, what I
said? Actuly I felt funny when he saw me
before, a feeling nothing to do with me but
outside. I am cheeting and lying. I have started

again after some hapenings. You write DIARY
after it hapens, but this one might be getting
there first.

BOY are you alright, you are tremmling.

ME I aspect I am cowld.

BOY have you got locked out of your house?

ME no, I have the quay.

BOY but you are not alright, you are unhappy.

Some of this is not excacly what we said, it
was more like: You look terible, has somthing
hapened to you? Do you want me to fetch my
mother? (~~no i want you to fetch mine but not
the exact Fran~~) But I do not put all that in
because I had not been rapid or anything.
Robin says that a clear mind will give the right
amount of detail, which is why pugns are the
wrong kind of detail.

ME I do not know what I am, thank you, I
shall know soon.

I had the note from Robin. DIARY is difficult
when the order of things overlapps, somtimes I
am thinking things that have not yet hapened,
and somtimes things have hapened and I am
not thinking of them, like the note, I did not
know what it said. I think it is importent to
have everything in the right place. Robin says
order is not the same as position. Fran said
position is nine points of the lawr. I never
worked out why Robin went insain then, Fran
must of said somthing true.

BOY well I must go now I have work to do, but I will come back later, I have been watching you all year, if you remeber I gave you a card at Xtmas. Look I will lend you this handky which is clean. Then he went away, and I didnt care but I didnt like it.

All that conversation looks like it was transalated from the french verbatim with an acsent. Now I will read the note, it will be in computor with acsent of Robin. VICT WHERE ARE YOU? IF YOU COME IN STAY BY THE PHONE. ALL IS WELL SO FAR. FRAN IS VERY WELL CONSIDERING. ROBIN. So far of ? what, and I am in or I wuold not be here. I tide Ambrosear to the camera(l) obscura(l) railings, it will eat grass, now I am in a chair again and the telaphone is not gowing.

But I am sitting by it. I wondre what I did today, I think I ran away. I have run away before, I remeber destinctly.

On a winter's day in the school holidays, the times when no one was working, because of University vacation and Fran's arrangement with her office, Robin and Fran went out without Victoria.

She was too young then to be left all on her own, so she went down to sit with Mr Paterson, Mr Pattypatty. That was what she called him then, by way of giving him a name, not because he patted her on the head more than most people.

'It's nothing personal,' said Fran, when she took Victoria to

131

Mr Paterson's door. 'She just hates you today, because she thinks she wants to come with us, but she can't, you know.'

'I know,' said Mr Paterson. 'She shall come in and play with the ornaments and talk to the budgies, and perhaps we can watch some television?'

'No cartoons,' said Robin. 'Unless they are instructional, but even they are distorted.'

'I'll come with you,' said Victoria.

'Not this time, Vict,' said Fran.

'A lot of reasons,' said Robin. 'Snow, very boring for you, and you wouldn't like it.'

'I like it anywhere,' said Victoria.

'Then you can like it here this morning,' said Fran. 'We shan't be long. I'm just going down to the hospital for a check-up.'

'I could go down to the hospital for a check-up,' said Victoria. 'They have children wards.'

'Not this kind you couldn't,' said Fran, smiling.

It was a smile about something untold; Victoria knew that clearly.

'Not this kind,' said Robin, but he was merely correcting Fran for saying a thing twice instead of once.

'I'm afraid she's going to be horrible,' said Fran. 'Little girls of eight often are.'

'Impossible,' said Mr Paterson. 'Impossible for her to be horrible. You see, I can be more horrible.' But it was only propaganda: he would put up with her.

Victoria had not planned anything, but everything seemed to go as if she had worked it out. Robin and Fran went. She saw them go along the road and round the corner. Then she felt quite at peace, and not inclined to be nasty to anyone. She liked Mr Pattypatty and his ornaments and the budgies, and she liked to play chess with the big chessmen. He always told her how to win, but occasionally she had caught him cheating and he had not succeeded in losing. For him to make her win was the same as winning himself, she thought.

Today she got halfway through the chess and then said she had to go to the toilet.

'I'll think what to do next,' said Mr Paterson, staring at the board, embarrassed by this wild incontinence.

'I'll go upstairs,' said Victoria, letting herself out of Mr Paterson's flat. She went up to the bathroom in her own flat, and while she was there she concluded that she could stay there on her own; there was no need for Mr Pattypatty to look after her.

For the moment these thoughts had nothing to do with being left behind or being angry about it. She had been left and that was a fact. She did not go down again. Instead she hid under her bed, with some centipedes of dust. Then it was obvious that no one was looking for her, and she came out. Mr Pattypatty would be waiting for her downstairs, but he would not look under her bed.

The rest of the flat was not interesting, until she thought of the secret upstairs room. Beyond the door to that there was a large empty narrow cardboard box, blocking the entry. She went past it and up the stairs. She was thinking of riding out into the snow on the rocking horse quite gently, since she had worn its joints very loose. Robin was not the sort to be able to mend it, and Fran could not even have thought about it.

She rode gently, and even so there was a lifelike clackety-clack from the rods and levers of the horse, and a sort of pitching wobble where something had come adrift. So it was a slow journey, not going far.

There were different things in this room at times. Once Robin had had a whole computer here for a time. The interesting thing about it had been the smell. It hadn't done anything, not even printing out. It had been helping Robin with vectors, which were nothing to do with vectorias, Fran said.

There was a different thing here today. Victoria put on her glasses, which were in her shirt pocket because she could play chess better without them. She saw a baby's cradle, draped and frilled and not new, but still unused. Victoria thought she had seen it before, and that it was something Wendy had grown out of, or decided against. But why was it in this secret room, hidden from Victoria herself?

She got down from the horse, and it went trotting on alone in its frame. She went to look in the cradle for occupants, babies. If Robin and Fran had accidentally got one she was anxious to see it, even if she was not meant to. If they were sneakily intending to have one she thought she should know as soon as anyone. Some people have a lot of them, but she had an idea that sometimes you got another because the other one was not what you wanted.

There was no baby, only rolled up crinkly cardboard.

But it was suddenly a colder day than even the weather showed. It was a day when she had not been told something known to the rest of the house.

'Are you all right, Victoria?' said Mr Paterson, from the front door of the flat.

Victoria had no answers now for other people. She was thinking only that her private life of being with Robin and Fran was threatened. Somebody else would be a good thing and she would enjoy a baby in the house. You take them walks. But it has to be shared before it gets in the cradle.

She came down the stairs. 'I'm just coming,' she said to Mr Paterson. First she had to go to her room and find a doll, take it up the secret stairs, and put it in the cradle bedded in corrugated cardboard.

Then she came down to Mr Paterson, into his flat, and finished the game of chess. She killed all his pieces, and several of her own, and then stomped his king into a corner and left it to die of starvation.

'You are very cruel,' said Mr Pattypatty. 'Would you like a biscuit?'

'Yes,' said Victoria, because it was herself she had slain, herself she had worked into a corner and left to perish. She put a pawn back on the board with her king. That pawn was the baby.

'Now you've really got me,' said Mr Paterson. 'That's a true win.'

Victoria moved his king and took the pawn. It was still right for it to be taken and laid with the other taken pieces in the cradle of the box.

I wish I didn't know, thought Victoria.

'You are dropping a lot of crumbs,' said Mr Paterson. She was eating with her mouth wide open and her lips drawn back. She felt dribbly, but dribbling crumbs is a difficult art. Mr Paterson did not like it. He was meant to think she was pathetic, but not to like her either.

Robin and Fran came back before lunch.

'No problems, I hope,' said Fran, coming in at Mr Paterson's door without knocking. Victoria ran to her. She was caked with cold and dewed with melted snow.

Smelling of hospitality, Victoria said.

'Of course he's happy to have you,' said Fran.

'No trouble at all,' said Mr Pattypatty, but that was not quite happiness.

No one asked Victoria about her problems. No baby had come back with them. She had to be carried up the stairs, because she was baby for now.

In the afternoon she went for a walk on the Downs with Robin. It was a fair bright day, and there was no wind. All over the slopes of the Downs children were tobogganing.

'I want one,' said Victoria.

'I used to have one,' said Robin. 'At the farm, I suppose.'

'The Welsh boys will be using it,' said Victoria.

'Wendy, too,' said Robin.

Then a kind Bristol boy let Victoria have two rides down the slope, while he emptied snow from each boot. She lost her glasses falling off at the end, and Robin had to dig for them.

Victoria ran away, without the glasses, while Robin scrabbled and thought of Wendy. She had seen, when she had the glasses on, that the Downs were full of people. She went to find them, running through the snow in a small field of clarity until others came into the circle with her.

Robin seemed to lose her. She had two more rides, and in one of them was at the bottom of a pile of other people and ended with a mouth full of snow. By the time she had sorted that out, swallowing and spitting, she had lost herself, and was even out of hearing of others. It grew dark, and it grew light again. It was part of another world to be walking about in the white soft ground with darkness and light coming and going under the street lamps.

Then they too went. There was only darkness and broken snow, and distant fuzzy suns showing indistinctly.

But it was peaceful. It was escape. She had got away and needed to consider nothing about Fran and Robin and cradles.

She began to make snowmen. The first she scooped up to almost her own height, in a patch of light from a window: there was a building here on the Downs, and she was close to its bright square star.

She made a row of smaller men, circling the building, going right round to a doorway. She knew where she was, and in daylight could have got home. She was not sure about managing in the dark with the path covered.

She went back and trampled the tall snowman into pulp. The king had melted. She kicked down her parade of pawns, winning that game, and came to the doorway once more.

There was no one about. It was a building you could go into. She went in. She heard Robin call to her, and she went on going in and up some stairs. She could see perfectly here, with close walls and light. She came up to a wooden place, and then there was a useless notice about the scenic view. She could see no view without her glasses.

She went into the dark place where the view was. She saw it. The view was lying on a table. She could see it, perfect and evident, every part of it. It was night, but she could see the street lamps and the light they cast on walls making the buildings visible. She walked round the view and it turned upside down. She bumped her head on a handle, and the view shifted. She walked about and about the table with the world on, and saw more than she had ever seen before.

Then Robin came, complaining about having to pay to get her from the Camera Obscura, which was where she was.

'And it isn't as if you can see anything in the dark,' he said, not bothering to look although he had paid looking-money. 'They should close it at nightfall.'

It was no good telling him that night was the best time, that night showed brilliant in the dark.

He was quite cross again at the bottom of the stairs, paying to get Victoria out, since she hadn't paid coming in.

Then he put her glasses on her and made her walk home cold. She did not mind. She could see. She could live for ever in the Camera Obscura, reading and eating all her needs from that table.

But Robin was at odds with her. 'She ran away,' he said, giving her harshly to Fran. 'Don't go near her. She smells, like a baby.'

But he had not been ridden down on by others on a toboggan. Victoria, the wet, expressive baby, was not ashamed.

Fifteen

DIARY (~~She~~) Fran did not have anything of that
baby. I dont surpose most of the time she had
me, it is unlikely to of had me on purpose,
fancy ordering a baby with glasses, no it is a
lie, I can remeber before glasses. I can remeber
so much I wondre how I could of done it all. I
remeber a minuet ago and years, back into
where there wasnt any thing, but it goes gently
into that part like not a hard edge, you begin
soft. I surpose it is soft for me and hard for
them, the remember of me beggining (~~if they ever
had~~) (~~if they ever had~~) finish this sentance. if
they ever had another, which is what I preseum
they are doing now. Actuly how cuold you do
such a thing, how cuold you sugest it to any
one.

But if they did, then what I am writeing is
praps they wuoldnt because so far I think it has
been Fran nearly died several times, not Robin,
that wuoldnt be any better any way, even if his
intalect is a little strange. Christ says he is my
dad, but we dont think like that. Christ says he
is not the famous outlawr of that name but a

139

dad like the one she has got, out all day in the car selling polices of insurrence, well Robin would never get there. Robin is more than that, he is a dr of knowledge. Even Fran is a spinster of knowledge, but I am the knitwit, I am the nobody of the world. The telaphone had not rung a single word. I am writeing out in advance of it, when it rings I shall write RING RING, in the middle of the other things. I wondre what the boy Paul is doing. I wondre what any body else is doing, all people are doing things. What is Mrs Fennal doing, is she feeding her duck or is she watching telavision like Mr Pattypatty and of coarse Christ, the reason of her square eyes. I have round eyes, the reason is of blue frames on my glasses not actuly the shape I am. Once there was

RING RING, RING RING. Enterupting.

ME hello.

PERSON Betty here, Im wondreing about my horse and my pupil, they did leave here long ago.

ME Ive got to stay by the telaphone.

BETTY is that Victorial? Where you been then. You dint ougt to go riding off like that never a word. I dont know what become of you, see.

ME I had to come home and there was no one in, so I have to wait by the telaphone.

BETTY you want to look after the horse, Victorial. Where is she now?

ME tide to the camera obscura eating grass.

BEETY oh yes, well bring her back soon, there little maid, she do like her own place of a night.

ME she will come back soon.

And then all the tara stuff. Robin says his thing and stops no taras or things, unless its Wendy. That wasnt him, he is still to come. Betty wants the horse first, not me. Once there was another horse, I can't remeber quite well, it must of been a long time ago, and wasnt here but it was after we came here from the rainy place. Problby my brane is full and things are slipping outy the other side, very likely. Cuold I of stolen a horse from school, baby school, primery school?

Victoria had been a mouse, a brown house mouse, in the infant pantomime. Miss Dogget had been apologetic to Fran about Victoria's state.

'She gets carried away,' said Miss Dogget. 'It's not quite like fancy, it's more as if a change had taken place. But all day long she has been this large mouse, and it hasn't worn off yet. Usually there is some return to normality after a time.'

'Not with that one,' said Fran. 'Come on, creature, let's have your pants down and see whether you've grown a tail.'

The mouse lost ears, tail, claws, teeth, squeak, and stood up, indignant.

'You have to set traps,' said Fran.

The mouse had not quite disappeared, however. It had, in the course of the pantomime, to change into a horse, and adopted that expedient now.

Victoria allowed so much to be known at home, but was not going to reveal the name of the story.

'Baffled,' said Fran. Even Robin, for once, did not seem to know, or he was not caring to join in. He was a bit thinky thinky that day, Victoria knew.

Not much mouse came from school. But with it came the horse part of the costume, a stick with a sock stuffed and tied to one end, with two button eyes and two felt ears.

That was Victoria's third self.

She had not been other creatures before. Even Miss Dogget could not know how fresh the idea was to her, and how she thought of nothing else for weeks, nothing else but being some animal.

Mouse was simple, even too simple once the part in the pantomime had been learnt. The part had not been enough, and the mouse continued. It was more than a horse that came home. It was a donkey in disguise, a spy from her world, with her in this other. Worse than that, it was a stolen horse, and there might be trouble on Monday when it was not there.

There were other things to be. On Saturday morning she was a dog, when they went shopping.

'What are you doing?' said Fran, the first time Victoria stopped.

'Woof,' said Victoria.

'Good dog,' said Fran. She had not realized that dogs stop at all posts and corners and even stationary bicycles. 'Have you got something in your shoe?' she asked, after waiting for Victoria twice more. 'Why are you standing on one leg? Vict, you are to stop it at once; don't you dare.'

'Dogs do,' said Victoria.

'Maybe,' said Fran. 'But you aren't. Just think, you haven't a collar or a licence, and if the dog catcher comes you'll be taken off to the kennel and we shan't know where you are and no one will want a dog with no fur. And lady dogs don't do that. Only gentlemen dogs lift their leg up.'

Some people continue to be dogs. When they came to the pet shop this one went in and tried on all the collars, even getting the man to fasten them on for her. 'It's a fine dog you've got there,' he said. 'Intelligent. Shall we sell it for you?'

'Yap woof yap,' said the dog. 'I need to go to the toilet.'

'House-trained too,' said the man.

'Really,' said Fran, when they were down the yard. 'You can't walk five hundred yards, can you? You should have gone before we came out.'

'Dogs don't,' said Victoria.

'They're right at school,' said Fran. 'You get carried away.'

In the afternoon they went to Wells, mostly because it was a fine day and not too busy a time of year. The back seat of the car was full of a large crow for most of the way. It built a huge untidy nest, and began to line it with Robin's hair tuft by tuft. He was not noticing, in a forbearing and tiresome way, waiting for Fran to sort out matters beneath the notice of the great thinker. Said Fran.

'Stop it,' said Fran, in the next breath. 'It isn't a robin's nest.'

'Just stop it,' said Robin. 'Is she pulling my hair out? Pull your own out. I'm thinking.'

'You're sulking,' said the crow.

Four miles further on Fran had to stop the car and see how

much of her very own hair Victoria had pulled. 'What a ridiculously silly thing to do,' said Fran. 'If you'd taken all that from one place you'd have a bald patch.'

'Or Robin would,' said Victoria. 'That's what I was doing first.'

'All sensible crows,' said Fran, 'start by being eggs.'

'What colour?' said Victoria, ready to be an egg.

'Blue,' said Fran. 'See whether you can hatch by the time we get to Wells. They take that long. Sometimes longer.'

Soon she had to stop again, thinking that Victoria was ill.

'I'm laying myself,' Victoria said, groaning. 'I'm a big egg, you know.'

'Five pounds nine ounces before plucking,' said Fran.

The crow hatched at Wells. It flew away before that, in fact, driven out by a hare in a field. Victoria had most trouble growing the ears, and until she felt she had that right she was content to remain still.

Then she hatched the flown bird, and was a hare. It was not difficult to take a hare along the streets. Now and then it went down on all fours. Victoria found it not easy to stay strongly in the skin of an animal she knew little about, and which could not speak or ask for sweets and pencils. Hares run across fields away from roads. They do not mix much with people. As well as that, Victoria's eyes kept coming round to the front of her head.

When they came to the cathedral she was ready to change into a cat. There was one there to model herself on. She knew several cats, and had no difficulty being one. It was so simple that she decided to be two at a time, and keep up a conversation.

One was Robin and the other Fran: they were being catty with each other. It was a good way of being able to think two things at once, and be in two places at the same time.

There is not much for a cat in a cathedral. There were no convenient mice, and all the cushions were too narrow to curl up on. Both cats became tired before Robin and Fran, but they had lasted longer than Victoria would have done all together and alone.

In one large round room, held up by a single pillar, the cats came to blows, had a circular fight, leapt about on the floor and shrieked and spat.

'This is too much,' said Robin. He went out of the room. Fran sat and watched until the fight was over.

'There was two of them,' said Victoria.

'I didn't know whether it was a fight or a fit,' said Fran. 'They scratched and they bit, till instead of two cats there weren't any. It's like that sometimes.'

'I aren't any,' said Victoria. Two minutes later she was very much taken by a couple of serpents being tamed, or led along, or killed, by some saints on some pillars that hung on a wall without touching the ground.

Robin said they were monsters, and had no reality like most of the substructure of religion.

'You don't have to come here to say so,' said Fran.

'I can go anywhere and say anything,' said Robin. 'It doesn't do much good to believe what you say.'

'And it doesn't stop me being one,' said Victoria. 'I am the largest one. I eat people.'

'Not me,' said Fran. 'I'm Christian. Eat the atheist.'

'I eat atheists,' Victoria shouted, and rushed away down the steps, shrieking, ravening, after Robin, who was walking away from this nestling.

The Christian lady caught her up and tamed the serpent with a shake. The atheist told it to behave itself. 'You've seen what happens to them,' he said.

'I think that's a joke,' said Fran. 'But I can't prove it.'

'I'm not making jokes, especially today,' said Robin.

'Why?' said Victoria.

'Just upset about work and things,' said Fran. 'You know how it is sometimes.'

Then they watched the clock strike the hour, the jousting knights on the carousel swinging round above the clock-face. 'All that is an early sort of computer, Vict,' said Robin. 'A computer of time and the phases of the moon. It's eleven days wrong.'

'Put another five p in,' said Victoria. 'I want it to go round again.' They had paid to see it, so she knew it worked for money put in.

They had tea in the town.

'Better now?' said Fran to Robin, looking into the pot at the bloated corpse of a catering tea-bag.

'No,' said Robin. 'It's still ridiculous. It's the old boy network. They'd arranged the post for someone they all knew. They practically promised it to me before I came to Bristol; and now someone has worked behind the scenes. Also, I might have stood a better chance if you'd been fitter. I don't mean I'm complaining, but it's a fact that if you'd only do the sensible thing at the right time you wouldn't be unwell, you know

146

what I mean, and I'd have less on my shoulders. That's got something to do with it, I know. Actually I suppose it's as plain as that clock-face in there; the way things are is set out; no room for new blood and fresh ideas.'

'But you're really grumbling at me,' said Fran, hoisting the body out on a spoon. 'And no one call tell the time from that clock-face, all clowns and phases of the moon. I know it's me. I've felt it all day. But you don't mean just about that, do you? You don't mean just that you didn't get the appointment. You mean other things too.'

'Another time,' said Robin. 'You began asking.'

'Because I can sense your mood,' said Fran. This time the tea bag hissed under artificial respiration and bled murky into the ash tray.

'For God's sake stop fidgeting,' said Robin. 'I don't have moods.'

But of course he did. He had slightly less mood after his tea, or coffee for him, and then they went home.

Before going to bed Victoria got out the rustled horse, rode its little stick and stroked its sock nose. No one was asking her to do anything, so she went on being the horse and its rider until Robin threw down his papers and told her for God's sake to be quiet and take that damned thing from between your legs, it isn't decent.

Fran had to put an insulted horse to bed, as well as an aggrieved rider. 'And to think,' she said, 'he doesn't even believe in God. Certainly not twice in one day.'

'Horses do,' said Victoria. 'Three times. Not cats, though, ever.'

On Monday morning the horse had dropped away behind the bed, and forgot to go to school. Victoria had to pretend to be herself being a mouse being a horse, until the next rehearsal, when the horse attended too. No one at school had missed it from its range behind the cloakroom door.

Sixteen

DIARY I cuoldnt ever manage of being my
favourite animal an (eriwigue) (erwg) (earwhig)
because of not getting my back legs up in the
air like the pinchers exept sometimes on a chair
and no one knew what I were. I dont know why
I didnt change into them because I thuoght
hard enough to of. It comes like a flash as if its
really you, I mean as if that you is the real
thing, I mean it feels more real than ordinary
reallyality, so which is actuly which, whats
there strongest or whats there most? It seems
silly to have questions in a DIARY because it
will never be an answer given. Praps I am
asking me to think, but its all I ever do. Robin
says we have to decide the limits of our
thinking but I go on thinking all ways and it
just goes on not quite real exept those bits that
are more than real. I excpect Robin was like me,
he had a rocking horse and a sledge and looked
in Grannys fire and saw things. I think. I can
ask him one day, I know he has come back even
if he has gone away again, but what is Fran
very well considering? I want to know. Actuly I

am getting this real feeling but not about being anything but about whether Fran is being anything, like is she staying alive, very well, considering being not alive. One time you do it too often, well, I cant see Fran being like Mrs Fennal, gone on for ever with a blown up leg. Mrs Fennal is actuly more real. Fran is just a part of me, Mrs Fennal is seperet. Being animals is seperet, so it is more real. How can we be real when we cant see our own face? How can DIARY be real to itself when it cant answer its own questions. I cant put question mark there, it would be ilogicall. My right arm is getting tired. My write arm is getting tired. My right arm is getting tired. I think I have done all my life including never haveing a kitten. A lot of computor paper has hapened today, 23rd.

RING RING, RING RING

ME hello.

ROBIN Vict, there you are.

ME

ROBIN Vict? Are you there?

I am not actuly saying things because I get out of breadth so he is saying hello again, are I there? instead of getting on with life and death I want to know, but I snork in my throte and say I can hear you.

ME I can hear you.

ROBIN great news.

ME yes what?

ROBIN you have a little brother.

Well actuly you wuoldnt get a big one, wuold I? The problem is for Robin to try and be logicall, he has to try hard.

ME what is its name?

ROBIN saying it any way, his name is (~~Adryon~~) Adrian.

He ways about one and a half gilligrams, he is in the (~~temperature~~) premature ward.

I was wondreing something like, wuold I have to bring him up, I think I cuold, why dosnt he say, so there was a gap in saying things.

ROBIN can you still here, are you there?

ME fine, I can hear.

Just say sumthing.

ROBIN well it took a long time but I got lucky at last there are going to be some changes.

ME what ones?

He is a sort of idiot man, Fran says, never tells you what there is. He is telling me about Fran I excpect, no, but he is talking about HEMPSTALL HEMPSTALL HEMPSTALL, not about Fran, which I want to know of most. I excpet I am saying ME yes and no and stuff.

ME yes and no.

I didnt hear it all to remember.

ROBIN we could move out to the country ect ect etc.

Ect ect ect is not verbatim, but how it went on, I put it in to give it the dramatac feel. In the

151

end I said,

ME what about Fran?

ROBIN (going on about HEMPSTALL H H and computorizing the chuck-outs) oh shes fine, quite comfortable. Then he is still talking about the country, leaving the universery, all exited of this baby, youd think hed had the pope or the daily llama, how people get it anounced to them, like Mr Pattypatty had fun of me once and got a pawn made queen with a carnation at chess the year it was a jubalee.

ROBIN I will wait and see Fran when she wakes up, she had this operation to get him out.

It was some sort of sexion, thats why they never said. They think I know everything and they think I dont know anything, but what Christ tells me is nonsens.

ROBIN it has been a long time and it wasnt easy. We used to tell you and it never hapened. You wuold go looking in all the cubpoards, and this time it hapened before we were ready.

ME is any one coming home?

I was hopeing they wuold go to the country and leave me, sort of.

ROBIN sit tight, Ill be home soon, Fran in ten days, and Adrian in a few weeks, hes very tiny.

ME like a bag of flower.

ROBIN the same weight but a difarent mass and volume.

I never know about mass and weight, but I surpose he means meat is heavier than flower and a baby is a difarent shape than a bag of holemeal or knocky knocky from HEMPSTALL HEMPSTALL HEMSTALL and problby HEMPSTALL, Adrian too.

ROBIN I shant be long, I want to tell her myself.

ME goodbye and stuff

and

~~ROBIN my good sensible daughter, now the famaly is compleet.~~

i dont know why i am uncompleet, i dont know why they cant go to the country when they have me, im just as real as Adrian. But of coarse you never know where you are with logic, not like sense. Then I wrote this to here and went in the kitchen and dride the knives, thats sensible but I dont know about logic, I wonder who got them started drying before. I got a feeling that I got smaller than my clothes so they dont touch me and keep me warm, so I washed my face and stoped feeling faint. Then I looked out of the window again, I often do, and theres the boy again, watchable over me, I think, and at this word I am going to go down and see about him, also Ambrosear.

'Next year we'll split the work,' said Dad. It was about half past five on a fine midsummer morning. 'Angela will be able to drive then, and you two can fetch and carry while I assemble.'

'Maybe we shan't have to get up so early,' said Angela. She was not complaining, but would rather have been in bed still.

'Just a long day,' said Mum. 'We'll leave those two little ones. They can make a night of it tonight.'

Tina was ready to go. There were four trailers beside the house, two of them in the garage, one in the drive, and a big one backed in among the roses. The rose bushes looked like a regular planting, but they had been arranged so that the trailer would park in diagonally. First to travel was the small trailer with a tent, some chairs, a kettle and other outdoor eating things.

The trailers had been brought up from Nailsea over the past evenings, ready for today. Today was worked out in all its details, and had been for some months. It began now whatever the weather, and it began in this way, whatever anyone's feelings; that is, all of them would work to the plan, even if full of fever or broken arms.

Tina started. She liked this sort of occasion, but possibly only because Dad had spent half an hour the evening before on a check of the transport system. She had spent the night in the road. Now she backed up to the first trailer, was hitched up, and they were off.

The journey was nothing, about a mile and a half, to the road across the middle of the Downs. Then they had to pull off the road on to a track, and across the grass to a place marked by nothing but a deliberate flatness.

To them all it was like arriving at a monument, or the site of the most significant event in history. They were alone. Paul got out, first man on the moon, and led the way to the hard standing, a place where concrete had been let into the grass. It was the monument to the Creasey family in fact, even if the fact was so insignificant that no one knew it except on the day when it was invisible. But here would stand the centre truck of the roundabout.

The first trailer was not for that place. It was commissariat first, Dad said, and this trailer held their supplies and shelter. Dad backed to the best place for it and Paul dropped the trailer off.

Mum often talked about sandwiches on this sort of occasion, but veered off towards roast and Yorkshire and two veg followed by apple tart and custard, all cooked on one gas ring at the back of a tent.

'Town girl, me,' she said. 'Don't like to rough it in old country places.'

Dad spent a few moments outside Tina, after switching the engine off. With that stopped there was only the pull of a morning wind against their ears. And the high song of lofted birds drifting down on them like honeydew. They were alone, with their long shadows pencilled on the grass, the sunlight running clear under Tina, her shadow standing on pillars, not wheels.

'Last bit of peace,' said Dad. 'You girls got all?'

'Should have,' said Mum. She began to unpack the trailer and set up her house and kitchen.

'Back in a minute,' said Dad. 'Ready, Paul?'

Paul was ready. This was the holiday day for him and them. This was the weekend when the roundabout revolved, the

155

Gallopers galloped, the merry-go-round merry went round; this was the riding day for Bristol at the Midsomer Fayre.

By the end of the first day Dad would be loading coins and notes into Tina, for the bank, and thinking he could give up his work and run the ride all the year. By the end of the second day he would be certain of it, and by the end of the third he would know that the whole of the next winter would be needed for maintenance, and the money would go nowhere. He would be tired of the succession of people, and deafened by the music the ride made with its steam organ. By the time everything had been taken down and packed into the barn at Nailsea he would have had his fill and want to be back to his work with the Post Office and the certainties of home.

'If your mum stops after this last one,' he said, meaning Tiny Wee as the latest baby, 'then in a few years' time I'll have no responsibilities and I can go on the road full time.'

Mum usually said nothing to that, but she had been known to say that a few months' wandering would suit her now.

The second, third, and fourth trailer came next, and were lined up in order. The fourth trailer, number seven, was really too big for Tina, and had always been too big for the Suspension Bridge. Dad and Paul had brought it round late one evening earlier in the week, on the long route past the docks, and miles up the Gloucester road to avoid the hills, and stood it among the roses. Now it was edged out, while Tina pulled, and the trailer resisted, before they got on their way. It had always been the worst part. Before Tina, this centre truck had to be hauled by a hired wagon.

The truck was put in place, and the supports let down.

'Lucky it isn't one of the real big efforts,' said Dad. 'We'd be putting this truck up on a bridge, and we'd have three great wagons. No, this dear liddle thing be plenty for us. But we ent done yet. You right there, Mother? We'll be off for the rest now, right?'

They went to Nailsea four times. There were five trailers there, but the fifth was the small one they would not need until last. It held spares and the music books, and there would be a time to come for it later, when the ride had been assembled, and tested, and when the bridge was open, since today it closed for a time.

Others were on the Downs when they came with the last trailers. These others were real showmen, who lived by their equipment, during the summer at least. They all said that the old breed was dying out, their sons would not follow them in the way of life. They thought that Dad had the right idea of how to carry the traditions on. The trouble was, they said, when they came across and gave a lifting hand or a spot of advice, the trouble was, that a good man at the fairground trade was really too good for it.

They came and drove in posts, and positioned wedges, handed up the swifts, and nodded with appreciation at work on the iron supports of the horses; and a one-legged stout man came to sit up with the steam engine, to light it for them if he could. He had an incantation about Magic and Welsh Brights, which went together for him, and his eyes glistened with delight.

Late in the afternoon Dad and Paul went for the last trailer. They had had to wait until the Midsomer Fayre Parade had crossed the bridge, since not only was the bridge impassable, but it was formally closed to traffic for two hours, whether the parade was on it or not.

They left the empty barn, closing its interior against the rest of the day, and came back over the Suspension Bridge. As they came off the bridge Paul saw the pink horse wandering and grazing up there beside and beyond the Camera Obscura, with its saddle on, like the horses of the ride, waiting for a rider; or perhaps having lost one.

Seventeen

DIARY I dont think I am writeing this for anyone now, I mean I am not the person that wants to hear about it any more, I am not interested in the history of my past or my today. How they dig things up is how I dont want to hardly any more, it can all get covered for ever, no one will ever know. I will get reprogramed, if it is a computor then it dreams wild dreams Robin says when they clean out the old programs. He says people work like that in fact, but I never heard of reprograming for people, so I now hereby invent it and will do it unto myself. Praps I shall have wild dreams, but actuly most dreams hapen becaus if they didnt how do we know what to dream.

I think that proves Robin is right. He must of struck the sense of things. I am sitting on (~~my thrown again~~) the grass again, thrown sounds like the toilet. It is not so warm, the sun is gowing. It would shine on my back but there are trees there. It shines on the bridge. Mr Pattypatty was wistling and getting his supper when I came down. When I came out it was

159

colder so I went up and got a coat. Actuly I got Frans (~~knight~~) knited one that she made with pockets and I have to roll up the sleeves, speckaly wool. Pens in the pocket.

BOY I like your jackit. I thought you wuold be coming out again because of the horse.

Actuly at that moment I have forgoten the horse, it belongs to the past, a wild program.

ME I wondre what to do with it.

For a moment we stood beside the horses memorial it left in the road, and he luaghed.

BOY (PAUL) there was once an elaphent at the midsumer faire.

Well it is strange he remebered that because I do as well, fancy knowing the same things, it is unlikely.

ME I had a ride on it.

BOY my dad is a fenatic on roses.

But I didnt quite hear what he said.

ME hadnt he seen a trunk before?

Then we explained about nose and rose, and luaghed, it was like knowing sombody, but when I laughed my stomack went grind grind like ringing its telaphone to me, and actuly hurt with hungeration.

BOY what are you going to do with the horse, are you going to take it back to Abots Lea?

Well, that is like seeing the same elaphent, knowing about Abots Lea and the horse.

ME do you know Betty?

BOY no.

That is not verbatim, it was a bit knocky knocky Betty who.

ME I have not decided.

It turns out he is Angela Creaseys (~~sister~~) brother, well he must be all right. I do not think I was quite nice, I am still on old programs, I was showing off, and that is amagenary like being a cat. I explained I was steupid somtimes but he did not listen to that. We unsadeled Ambrosear. Now she is part of the old time I can see it is a patcient horse and not hapy to be left tied to the railings of the camera obscura. I went down and wrote the spelling because I can do better in fact I can do best and I WILL, I will win the spelling Olympycs gold meddle if they have them any more. Robin says I am a fenatic speller just like it sounds. We put the saddle inside the gate.

Now the boy has had to go. I am writing this out here in the light but I said I wuold be in the camera obscura, it is open, and he will come back. Well, Fran cant come back and I trust him more than Robin. The camera obscura is open because they are having candlight suppers in there, it is very costly, the door is open and I know the way, you arent excacly meant to. Ambrosear is at another part of the railings, she had eaten all those before, grass I mean. Now I am up in the camera obscura and taken off my

161

glasses. It is not dark in the gallery, only in the picture bit. I am gowing to stay here until there is a light in the house and Robin is back. I can see the house (~~distintly~~) clearly, but I can see the other way if I swing the picture round and right across the Downs there is the postcard thing, and I can hear it too. Here are two words I spell alike but they are difarent, distint and distint, one means far off and the other means clear and, and this is both. It is the midsummer faire and it is the merygorounde of the boys card, I excpect it is an intarest of his.

I have decided that I will not wear these glasses any more, they are blue plastic frames, horible, but free, however I shall never wear them again, I am gowing to have gold ones imediatley, blue is programed out. My stomack is smelling the suppers they have down there, (~~delic~~) lovely candles and saintly wine. Once they were happy. Fran said she can tell a hock from a Hempstall (where she buoght it), they were drinking it. Robin said the pugn was enough to make him leave whome. I didnt get it. Paul had not bruoght any thing to eat except a mint I do not like and a piece of chalk. I have had another look at the faire. They wuold have hambrugers there or toffee apples. I can tell by the music.

She had been inside the music once, back in memory, after tea, instead of going to bed, Robin and Fran not saying where they were taking her, or indeed that they were taking her anywhere. She had felt slightly like some other person, just outside her own self, and having problems with its tea, remembering its school dinner.

The music had been growing louder. Victoria had been thinking it was better than seeing. If the thing you were going to would always sound at you, you would have no problems. She was having no problems today in any case, holding hands with Robin and Fran. The music came and went a little as the wind lifted and dropped it.

Fran thought she was over-excited, and that not eating her tea was a sign of it. But Victoria had had the small twisted feeling before knowing they were going to the Midsomer Fayre.

Robin had been under-excited. 'I suppose I had better come,' he said, 'though there is not much point in observing the well-known imbecilities of country life.'

'Some people,' said Fran, 'have talked a lot about living in the country one day when they get Head of Department or a similar post. Or.' She did not explain what 'Or' was.

'Merely as a healthy place to live,' said Robin. 'Not to know people or take part in things.' Something was Fran's fault again.

'Of course you would have to take part,' said Fran. 'You're just feeling superior to people who enjoy fairs, you left-wing elitist.'

Victoria jogged away between them at a lower level. Her glasses had been left at home so that they would not be lost. She would be able to see enough, Fran said.

Her hands were getting sticky, but when she let go of either

163

side she felt that the ground was going away from her and there was nothing to balance by, a sort of one-sided dizziness.

There were some nasty smells coming. 'I expect you'll have to fill up on hot dogs,' said Fran. 'You can, for once, if you like.'

'It smells like the Refectory on an off day,' said Robin. 'Or the small animal house at the zoo.'

Then all at once, for Victoria, there stood, on its own, in the middle of the plainest blur possible, a veritable, veridical elephant, walking towards her. To Fran and Robin it was much more part of the Fayre, and they could see the stalls and booths beyond, and the rope fence to make a clear walkway. Victoria saw the green grass surrounding the elephant, a radiant mixture of reds behind it, and above it the blue-white skies.

She ran to it. It walked to her. The end of the great trunk scanned her and read her and left her, or perhaps sucked some of her away. The creature turned round about her and walked off. Its back was covered with children, who were saying, Eh, innit good eh? and Hey mister thee bissent taken we far enough.

In its trunk the elephant carried a record of Victoria. When it had walked itself off she sat down, being dizzy both sides now, and still a little twisted in the middle. She was prepared to sit and wait for it again.

'We thought you were going to be trampled to powder,' said Fran, but she did not mean it as a fact, only as something that could be thought.

Victoria put the Fayre together in her own way, piece by piece. She could not understand why anyone should want to know already what was there; she did not want to go straight to anything, but had to look at each booth and stall, at the marvellous glitter of things to be given away for trifling deeds of skill or common and universal luck; great pink bears free for a few pennyworth of knocking down wooden targets; dolls spotless and new under film ready to be owned by those with a simply faculty for dropping a ring on a stick; fish that swam serenely in plastic bags available for the art of throwing balls in the throats of gaping clowns. Riches could be gained for next to nothing.

'You can afford all this,' said Victoria, working out the notices and studying the know-how needed. A large pink bear would hold her upright, she thought, and might take away a metal taste she now had in her mouth, and keep her warm in the wind.

Robin afforded what he could. 'Alas,' he said, 'I have never assimilated the necessary co-ordination of hand and eye.'

Victoria found him something he could manage, a game that said it was a computer and an electronic brain. The prizes were big plastic beach balls, but better than nothing.

Robin did not win. He was above mere machinery. 'It isn't a computer,' he said. 'It's just flashing lights when the ball comes down and makes contacts. I didn't accumulate enough score.'

They went through the hall of mirrors, and the hall of terrors and waxworks, where a waxwork came to life and jumped out at Fran. Victoria liked that as well as anything because the shock drove away her own funny feelings. After that they got themselves lost in the looking-glass maze, where you could not tell how to turn in order to get out, because everywhere you looked was everywhere already.

'It makes you think about what you mean by destination,' said Robin. 'This is more like reality than reality itself.'

There were rides, slides, and whirls. Robin took her on a dodgem. 'I can drive naturally without anxiety,' he said. But Victoria had to get off in a little while, not because of the bumps and crashes, but because of the changes of direction.

'But you're a good traveller,' said Robin. He went on to be a bad driver. Fran and Victoria stood at the side and watched, heard, and smelt, the sparks at the floor and netted ceiling of the rink.

There was a helter-skelter slide, a spiral that had to be climbed first. Victoria went up and found the ground had gone from view, and she had to push off without knowing where she was bound, and without the mat she should have sat on, so she had a sore ride over bolt-heads.

Now she could not stand because of headache and dizziness, or sit. Fran thought they should go home, but Victoria thought not, that she could continue to enjoy herself enough to override any discomfort; and Robin had argued himself into thinking the Fayre might be a proper subject of interest to him. He wondered whether the precessions of the Giant Starwheel might not have something to say, and went off to try them.

'At the end of one of those swings he'll come sweeping off into the crowd,' said Fran. 'He'll hate that.'

Victoria stood in the queue for the elephant ride. She recovered her balance a lot there, but felt empty down the spine. The lumbering of the elephant, when she was on it, suited her. The ground had gone again, and swimming into view was the tip of the animal's trunk, coming up to check on the man in charge; another creature entirely from the elephant.

'Now we can go home,' said Fran. Victoria went to the front of the elephant, wanting to own and control the trunk, the magical understanding thing, being itself.

Victoria had a ride on the roundabout. Here she was closest to the music, which came out of the middle of the rings of horses. She was up on a white one, clutching a gilded spiral pole. But when the horses started the music hardened into mad pounding and she was overwhelmed. The horse leapt and swooped, it swung to one side continually, her fingers would not join on the post, and she slid off on to the platform. The horse trod up and down over her, its feet coming and going.

Victoria put her head down and had all the agony of being sick without anything happening except the taste, which she swallowed down again, malty and fermented like cornflakes, or like Grandpa's cold tea in a glass some nights.

['Not for me,' said Fran. 'Not whiskery,' Victoria remembered. Tickling my back.]

Now, under the horses, she thought she had died and fallen from the ride to heaven, but remembered not to tell Robin.

The woman who had been running the ride from the centre had lightly come across to her, picked her up and stood with her, one hand resting on the bobbing horse, until the ride slowed and stopped.

Fran was there too, in a moment. 'Not used to riding,' said the woman. 'You want to have another turn, dear?' she said to Victoria.

Victoria shook her head, and the ride started up again.

'We'll go home, I think,' said Fran. 'Thanks all the same.'

167

'Big fat woman,' said Victoria, in a moment or two.

'Not really,' said Fran. 'Going to have a baby before long, that's all.'

A baby elephant, thought Victoria, would put its trunk out first to see whether the bed was made. How could I think that thought?

She walked home feeling very woolly, walking on soft ground with soft feet, lumpily. Then she sat on a chair at home, keeping her head still, feeling hot and cold in turns and at the same time, and the windows went black now and then.

'Bed for you,' said Fran.

'No,' said Victoria, moving only her mouth, no more of her head. But in a little while Fran picked her up and laid her on her bed, undressed her and put her into it. The elephant could not put out its trunk to see whether it was made. There she lay and came in and out of the swirls of the Fayre and still heard the music drifting on the breeze in and out of the window. She was getting the measles, said the doctor next day, the medicine doctor; not a knowledge one like Robin, really knowing nothing.

Eighteen

DIARY It is getting dark. I am hungering. Actuly
a lot is hapening in its way, first the sun
gowing red, in that direction is the faire and its
lights are on, they were before I think but now I
can see them. Why am I writeing this, the
program is still in place, praps it is impossable
to wash it out, I cuold get clean. I remeber
when our form got the scouts book, a clean
mind in a clean body it said, and Christ said
once a week is enough and we knew she didnt
mean a bath a week and every body luaghed
but we didnt know what we did mean not actul
knoledge you get marks for in a test.

Well, praps I havent got a new program yet,
and of coarse the old ones dont go away, but
where do they lead? I am like Robin, saying
they do not lead anywhere but its all we have.
Fran says it leads to here and thats all weve got
but it isnt the same, it goes somwhere, revealed
religion says so. Robin says you will never make
a computor (~~conc~~) (~~consui~~) see itself, like my
DIARY wont, so humanity, or manity and
womanity wont get beyond itself. (~~The sun~~

169

~~went red~~) I did that bit. It is pretty in that direction. Next Robin is home, there is a light in the house, I saw it in the camera obscura. However, when I looked again it was darker and too many other lights were on. And I can not see any other way. I am not wearing my blue glasses again.

I shall write to Fran. I will use one of her jokes. I will send her parsley because I cant aford lettuce. It means I will send parcels because I can not aford letters. Another instant when Robin went insain. I dont know why he bothers. He does think of liveing in the country. Perhaps it is his old programs but it cant be, he never lived at the farm when he was little, Grandpa only got it when he got to be a sir of honour of the queen. Wendy cuold be a lady if she married him. I have just had a cold feeling of knowing that Granny was a lady of honour and I didn't ever think of it, well it didnt suit her, she was born a plain widow. Fran will be ashamed of me the relation of honours not able to spell, but quite neat writeing, like Robin's.

Also what shall I write. I can only think of another of Fran's jokes, I will tie up a loop of (~~spagety~~) (~~spaghetthi~~) spaghetti and send her a spaghet-me-knot. The fathers dont bring babies home, I am sure. Besides it is in the thing they keep them in, I surpose it is like a pettri dish to hold a kilo and a half. The page is getting darker. I wonder where the boy is. Far away? I think he went to the faire. Fancy knowing the elaphent. I do not know what to do in the dark, which isnt yet, I can see the pages. I have got to do somthing with Ambrosear, Betty will want him. I think I have been like Robin and Fran, going out without saying, but I had no reasons, Ambrosear isnt having a fole. I shuold not of gone riding, I shuold not of come back. I should of said I wanted a donkey with blue bedes, not a strawbury rowan.

'People who don't ride call it red,' said Louise. She was at her desk drawing a horse. 'We call it a light bay. Hannah, come and draw the tail for me. You always make it look so life-like.'

'It's an accident,' said Hannah. 'I have no interest in horses at all.'

'Perhaps you can't afford it,' said Louise.

'We're saving up for a unicorn,' said Hannah. 'You just draw them like that, they stick out from the body a bit and then hang like a dress. It isn't difficult.'

'Thanks all the same,' said Louise. 'Fourteen hands, light bay. He is called Cantata.'

'All horses look like that,' said Christabelle. 'Don't they, Wendy?'

'They all look the same to me,' said Victoria. She was polishing her glasses at the time so she did not see the others waving to her to stop talking: someone was coming in at the classroom door.

'Order point, Wendy Hempstall,' said Angela Creasey, the prefect on duty. 'By way of interest, what look all the same?'

There was some giggling about what could all look the same, some muttering Bosoms, and others Prefects.

'All be quiet,' said Angela. 'You can have as many order points as I like, and I can give as many as you like. It's up to you. Get on with your work, Wendy.'

Angela went away then.

'And that drawing just sitting in front of me,' Louise muttered triumphantly. 'She never looked, she was on to Wendy most of all. Cantata has a half-brother called Oratorio who won a race last year.'

Angela Creasey? thought Victoria. He's called Paul. Paw.

'Kindergarten fathers' egg and spoon, no doubt,' said Hannah.

'At Cheltenham,' said Louise. 'They sold him. They do that, if you win a race they sell the horse. They don't if it lost.'

'How much did they get?' said Christabelle.

'Oh, I don't know,' said Louise. 'We don't talk about money. Cantata cost me three hundred and sixty-five pounds. I paid all of that myself. I owe the rest to my dad.'

'Mine was just given to me,' said Victoria, astonished at prices, and startled to think that horses were bought and sold. She had some idea that they continued their own existence by being given, or giving themselves. Ambrosia seemed to have something to do with the farm, and something to do with Betty, and with herself, but was her own financial manager, with Grandpa buying the hay.

'You haven't got a horse, Wendy,' said Louise. 'Of course you haven't.'

'But she's saving up for a centaur,' said Hannah.

'I didn't really want it,' said Victoria. 'It just got given. It's called Ambrosia.'

'I expect it's some old retired pet one,' said Louise. 'It's got a sort of grocery name.'

'It's an ordinary one,' said Victoria. 'A girl.'

She was the only person in the classroom who would have referred to a female horse as a girl. Everybody but Hannah laughed at her, partly for saying the wrong thing and partly for saying she had a horse at all.

'Only stable boys say colt or filly or mare,' said Hannah kindly. 'Ordinary people say boy or girl, the queen says lady or gentleman. Unicorns are different. We shall get instructions with ours. It'll be a viscount at least. Possibly majesty.'

'But go on,' said Louise, 'have you truly got a horse?'

Victoria was unable to say any of the right things about its height or colour. Betty had talked about hands, but how many there were she had forgotten. Even the colour, an odd one, escaped her mind. She guessed at butterscotch fir, and that seemed not to have been heard of.

But there was a reasonably satisfactory time when Louise, who was jolly as well as being a snob, got out in front and rode an imaginary horse for Victoria's benefit, and a totally happy moment when Angela came into the room in the middle of it and missiled out another order point. But since the bell rang as she gave it, Louise was able to continue her horseplay.

'They didn't believe that,' said Christabelle, in the school yard afterwards. 'Look, there's Angela's boy friend, isn't he little?'

'It's her brother,' said Victoria. She thought a brother would walk up like that, hand something over, and then go. Brothers and sisters forget they are other people to each other.

'You've got in a way of saying things,' said Christabelle. 'Like about a horse. You would of told me, because we see each other on Saturdays, and you ring me up sometimes. You couldn't of kept it to yourself. I couldn't, so how could you?'

'You'd like a horse,' said Victoria. 'I didn't.'

'Oh Wendy,' said Christabelle. 'You and Mrs Fennal are strange people. Dynamite and butterscotch, no wonder no one believes you, you haven't got the words right at all.'

A fact is a fact. Robin often said so. But some facts cannot be demonstrated: Ambrosia stayed as a fiction with all the class but Hannah, who said she would know just as much about any horse she owned; and possibly she owned a whole stable of them but had forgotten the details: possibly they were caterpillars being trained to hatch. 'The family fortune is entirely founded on butterflies,' she said.

Truth was not enough. Ambrosia's actuality was not made more likely when it was known that Wendy lived in a flat in the middle of Clifton. Victoria embarked on some deceit, partly because of Ambrosia, and partly because she had begun to dislike getting home more than an hour early, unable to settle to homework, restless and wanting to be with people in some other place; though not at school. Sometimes she had telephoned Christabelle, but her mother had asked her not to, because Christabelle was to do her homework then.

Once she had telephoned Hannah, but Hannah had talked without respite for a long time about some imaginary set of beings and people she said they both knew, Mrs Osborne and

Georgie, quite strange to Victoria. Victoria had hardly been able to join in the game, and concluded that she had been put off on purpose and got rid of; talked out. But even talking on the telephone was a hollow act; she wanted something else.

Disbelief in Ambrosia, which she could not blame them for, because she had been unconvincing, led her to try to impress the class with other unbelievable things. That is, she knew they should not be believed, and what others did with what she said was their affair, though she knew what the effect was.

The effect was that they didn't believe her. She knew she was acting out something unreal, but knowing about it was real, at least. It's only the same as Louise's Cantabrother, she told herself, because she felt that possibly the drawing was the only thing real about that horse.

'Our actual house is in the country,' she said. She thought about putting it near Chepstow, where the farm was, but she did not like to confuse herself, or remember the Welsh hills in the background as part of a stage set. 'We just have the flat for the weekdays.' Whether anyone heard her say it she could not tell. She was hardly telling them; she was telling herself.

What happened was that she walked down to the Centre with Christabelle once or twice a week, and while Christabelle caught her bus home, Victoria got on any other passing one, took a twenty p ticket, got off after a few corners and walked home, through streets and squares she did not know, up alleys and steps that were strange, and by waterways that wandered uncharted. Once she even passed below the Suspension Bridge and walked the crowded Portway and up the long hill.

Then in the Centre one day a hand closed on her arm.

'What are you doing down here?' said Fran, voice and hand like iron on her.

Victoria looked at the dock brimming with water. She had nothing to say. Fran took her back to her office, imprisoned her on a stool in the waiting room and told her not to move. When the office closed they walked home.

'Do you want to say anything?' said Fran, after half an hour of hard silence.

'No,' said Victoria. 'It wouldn't add up for you.'

'Mock total soup,' said Fran. It must have been a joke.

The next day, as Victoria was going out of school, she was called back by Angela Creasey. With her conscience clear Victoria stood at the bottom of the steps and looked up at her. Now came Fran's scolding; here were instructions from school about going straight home, or staying in until Fran called for her. Victoria felt herself stare and stare unblinking, until a cold-weather tear fell down her face and she went away.

On some trifling occasion, to do with leaving shoes about, probably, since they all did that, she was caught in the same place, on a rainy day, by Angela. This time she looked at the ground, and saw the flashing lamps of the school warning sign reflected in the wet tarmac. Paul had been there both times. He must have been a brother to come a second time, after hearing Angela the first time.

Later Victoria wondered whether he knew she was that scolded child.

Often on the days she might have borne to be at home she had to go riding. She walked across the bridge to the bus and went on that the mile or two along the road. One day she went down to Betty's, after Fran's special lunch and a special joke about Gnocchi, gnocchi; who's there? Pasta; Pasta who? Pass da parmesan. Robin had been severe about word-play, and the distress it caused to him and the confusion it brought to accuracy in language. Fran had not minded his response.

Victoria had taken Ambrosia out alone. Her solitary ride was intended to be round the three lanes and back to the stable. Betty sometimes asked her to make a little trip on her own, more or less within call. 'I could be looken, mind; likely.' Today Victoria made a bigger trip and went further, coming down a quiet road to the Suspension Bridge, with nothing in mind but to go across and talk to someone, because the solitary riding was as bad as the solitude of afternoons when school was over. The road was quiet because the Suspension Bridge was closed. The gate was across the carriageway.

'Sorry,' said the keeper, 'you'll have to wait a bit.'

Victoria did not stop. She guided Ambrosia over to the left, and hurried her along, the canter being something she could do easily now, across the bridge on the footway, dizzily over river and road now she was high on the saddle and had her glasses on. Ambrosia had got into something like a gallop towards the end of the bridge, and the man there, who had been ready to stop her, had stood back. Then she had swung up on to the Downs, and gone to the house.

Nineteen

DIARY I can see the town better now on the table. It is a hollow table, in the basin of it my glasses are lying. They make a dimpal in the picture, that is how they think things are. I am useder to the dark, and I can see walls and roads not just lights. The faire is prety. The bridge is dreamy. I am pure hungry now, not in pain of it can sic you. Actuly, I have changed, I am indapendant. They have still got a child, that is their lookout and I have got my lookout too. They cant improve me any more, this is what I am going be, on my own, and think my own thinks. Actuly thuoghts have been thuoght before but if it was all by another person that person wuold still be you, but you didnt have the same things happen so it isnt you or the same thuoghts. This is the last day I will write DIARY in any way, 23rd June. Now I am not a child any more. I will stay out all night tonight. If I had decided that before I wuold of left a note. But I cant go and take one, Paul will be coming back. I have a fealing he might bring a pink baer with him, I will call it Bruinel after

the bridge. Now I am outside again. Paul has
come again. I was sitting in a chair because he
apeared in a beeholding manner sudennly, not
very visable. Then just after him came the
woman of the obscura. It is too dark to write
down our verbatims but she sent us out, she
disproved us, we have come out. Paul says he
will get me somthing to eat from the faire. I will
stay here, I have also got Ambrosear, the
woman sending him away. Then when she had
finished all the lights inside she bruoght a
buckit of water and she drank it. Ambrosear
did. We should not have a valuble horse like
that, and I said we wuold take it back. I do not
think it cost 365 pounds but a valuble Grandpa
might of paid it. I cuold sell it and buy a house.

Nobody should see this. I really know how to
spell. I really know the words. I was screaming
to myself all day, being a baby, but with no one
there to tell me anything or hold me or even
ignore me.

This is the last page of DIARY. I am under a
lamp to write by. I can see by it and understand
things outside the light. I am a new snake,
casting off my old eyescales. I can see in and
out better. I think I was meant to get here. If I
wasn't I wouldnt think about it. It all adds up,
not like mock turtle soup. Things actually
happen in a muddle, but all at once you get out

of the spaghet-me-knot, and here I am. I am
happy under the lamp with the place nightlike
round me. I understand everything now. I think
this is how I was meant to be, I think I um
programmed. I am   Here is Paul.

'You want to be wandering off at this time of night?' said Mum. 'I'm not sure about that, Paul.'

'It's his woman,' said Angela. 'She must be somewhere around.'

'She shouldn't be either,' said Mum. But she knew Angela was in charge and had more authority. 'This time of night,' she added, going away from the ride and to the car.

'Enjoy your time when you can,' said Dad. 'But not many free rides on our Gallopers, and not back late. Mum and I are going home to sleep, and we want you to keep an eye on things here.'

'Yes,' said Paul. He was tired. He had lived a long day, driven a great distance, hauled a huge amount, walked across the Downs three times, nine miles walking perhaps. 'I shan't forget.'

'Don't be short of cash,' said Dad, dipping his hand in the box and giving him a fistful of coins and notes.

'You'll be around, will you?' said Mum, with Tina's door open.

'Yes,' said Paul. 'I'll fetch her first.' It had not come to his mind what to do, after pledging himself to go back to the Camera Obscura. But of course it was clear that girl and horse should come to the Fayre; there was nowhere else to be.

He went across the Downs again, away from the light and crowd and clamour, into the dark and peace of the small wind.

He was mistrustful of Victoria's ability to stay at the Camera Obscura; he thought she was bound to have been taken, or merely gone, home by now.

He came up the steps quietly. At the top the lights were out, and he had to wait a moment to see whether she was there. He saw her on one of the benches, waking. Behind him the custodian of the building came up and asked them to leave, and to remove their horse. Best go home, she said. Victoria said she would take it home.

'Do you want to come to the Fayre?' said Paul.

'Not really,' said Victoria. 'I've got to take the horse back. But I am mostly hungry.'

'The horse has to go to Abbots Leigh,' said Paul. 'Right? Well, that's the other way. I'll go back to the Fayre and bring you something, and then I can go with you to Abbots Leigh, and then I have to go back to the Fayre.'

'What for?' said Victoria.

Then they both thought she was stupid. He knew he was not justified in thinking so, because how should she know about the Gallopers; she knew she was stupid, because it came clear to her that Paul and a roundabout, and a roundabout and the Fayre were closely tied together: she had not connected the roundabout with its master, or the need for it to have one, that was all. Roundabouts, like horses, ran their own affairs, jogging a predestined track.

'I live there,' he said equally stupidly. 'No, the family is there with the ride.' He wanted to say that it was that music they heard, but at that moment the ride was between books of it, Carolina,'. . pig . .'.

'I understand,' she said. 'I didn't know it was logical, that's all.'

'Dad's really,' said Paul. 'But we all do it.'

He went across the Downs again, filled with the gladness of caring for her, of being the only person caring this night, joyful at the thought of bringing her objects she needed. Fish and chips. His legs were tired. He kicked his own ankle crossing some rough grass.

His delight turned to anxiety before he got to the Fayre, and to a fret as he stood in the line for the fish and chips. He could not bear to stand-and-wait, but had to go at once and see that Victoria was still there and still all right. He left the line, and ran off into the darkness again. He was well into it before sense returned to him, and he walked again to the line and rejoined it. But again he had to leave it and stand there in anguish, apart from the rest of the world, and feel the inadequacy of his single presence, in one place at a time, when he wanted to be in more than one of each. Again he joined the line, and this time he stood to the end. Quit ye like men, he thought from the saint of his own name, be strong; and with helmets of salvation and breastplates of righteousness in mind, bought the fish and ran out into the dark again, late, time wasted, but sustained by having been mad.

She was under a street lamp, up among the bushes by the Camera Obscura.

For them both there was a strangeness about the actuality of an almost midnight meal, one under the faint light of a fallen sun. The Downs lie quiet and deserted to the distant Fayre. Ahead of them there sink the dark depths of the gorge, and hung in a hazed bow of light, the Bridge, lit on its far side.

Above, summer stars blink; music comes from far away.

When they had finished Paul said, 'You must go home.'

'Not tonight,' said Victoria. 'They can do without me now. They've got a new baby.'

'We do that too,' said Paul. 'Quite often.'

'They haven't done it before,' said Victoria. 'They have tried but not succeeded. I thought all day that Fran had died of it, because she nearly has before.'

'Fran,' said Paul. 'Who's that?' And then remembering the name from Christmas Day in church, I'm Fran Hempstall.

'Fran and Robin,' said Victoria. 'Parents. But I'm giving up that sort of thing now, being a child, I mean. They got another this afternoon, called Adrian, without any warning. I think they gave up saying anything because of bringing bad luck, though Robin doesn't believe in that sort of thing. He does computers, and says that chance and luck are statistical evidence only of consistency.'

Paul worked it out. 'But there is luck,' he said. 'He must be thinking of something else.'

'You should tell him,' said Victoria. 'I think I have to take this horse back. Have the men on the bridge changed shift? This afternoon I came across when it was closed, and they might know me, with a pink horse.'

Ambrosia was content to be saddled again. Victoria got up, and Paul walked beside. No one challenged them on the bridge. Horse and rider went through free, the man at the gate waving Paul on as well.

They went out into the countryside, one, two, three miles, and there was the gateway of the stable. At first they had talked, and then they had trudged. Now, at the gate, they unsaddled, dropped the saddle in the cart in the open shed, and put Ambrosia where she spent the summer nights, in the paddock at the back. Then they left.

It had been unromantic and wearying. But they were lucky now, or consistency was playing tricks. Paul was wondering how his heels would walk all the way to Clifton again, how his calves could flex and reflex those thousands of times more. Then a late bus came along the road, reading BRISTOL on the board, and they waved it down, though they were between stages and stops. They rode to the bridge.

'Wait a minute,' said Victoria, gazing at the gorge she could not see. 'I am going to end my life.'

'No,' said Paul, alarmed. People jump from the bridge.

'No,' said Victoria. 'My old life. I am going to throw away all that childness. This is my Diary, all this bundle of computer paper. But first I shall throw away my glasses.'

They stood on the lee side of the bridge, on the downstream walkway. Victoria pulled the blue-rimmed glasses from her pocket, opened them, and hurled them into the gulf of darkness, into that ribbon of road and river: they could choose as they fell down the wind, see for themselves, two miles down.

'Plastic,' she said. 'I shall have gold ones henceforwardly. Next the Diary has to go. The wind will take it away.'

She shook out the long roll of computer paper, sheet after sheet, until it trailed away out of her sight, fluttered by the wind tugging at it.

'Book music,' said Paul.

Sheet by sheet the perforations tore, went away. Before they had all gone she took out her own pen and wrote:

> DIARY It is getting totally dark. I am with Paul.
> We are on the bridge.

She let the sheets go, and cast the pen, all Fran's pocket of pens (that included some of Fran herself), after it.

That was that. She held Paul's arm, fiercely for a moment, more yielding and responsive than the iron rail of the bridge.

The Fayre was in full cry when they came over the bridge. As they crossed the Downs the flare of it dimmed before them, the lights died, and a second dusk fell on the ground.

Paul stopped. 'I'd better take you home. Shall I?'

'No,' said Victoria. 'I'll stay at your house, or something. I'm going to be out all night. I don't belong to them like that any more. I threw everything away at the bridge.'

Paul was worried when he came to the Fayre. He had not thought of bringing anyone home to stay, nor was it in fact home; moreover he had done it not by charm or endeavour or intent, but by untimely accident.

He did not want to have done that. He had wanted the stars and the magic city, and for his feet not to ache so much, and everything to have been intended by him, not by fate or chance or accident. But he was lucky again in not having to account for anything. Mum and Dad had gone back to the house. Angela was sitting up in the tent making cups of chocolate for Martin and Tiny Wee, who would not go home and were still awake, troubled by nostalgia.

Victoria felt her old life creeping up on her when she saw

Angela. But this was a different Angela, more like a gypsy, kneeling at midnight in a tent on the Downs, balancing a pan of milk on a gas ring, surrounded as a mother by Martin and Tiny Wee. Marion, thought Paul, his head ringing with day, detached, alien. I shall change too and call her Marion.

'You look different without your glasses, Hempstall,' said Angela. 'You should be at home.'

'I've run away for the night,' said Victoria.

'You can sleep on the ride,' said Angela. 'It's just boards. Show her, Paul.' No order points.

When the ride had stopped a huge canvas curtain was hung right round it, made of many pieces. It had been one of Dad's large expenses, having to be bought made, hemmed and eye-leted. Paul undid a couple of toggles and showed the interior. There were dim bulbs glowing in the canopy run from a battery, enough to work by if needed, enough to watch by, if there were vandals.

Victoria sat on the floor, out of the midnight wind at last.

'Not very clean,' said Paul. 'I'll get a blanket for you. There isn't anywhere else to be. I should take you home.' But he was swaying with weariness and a day many hours too old.

'No,' said Victoria. Then, when the rug came she lay down and pulled it on to her and closed out the day, all her old life, her childhood and the past.

Paul wrapped a blanket about himself and sat on the steps. The day throbbed through his head, until the head was too heavy to hold. He laid it on a higher step, and slept where he was as the sky lightened to another day.

Twenty

The sun came round under the back of the Downs during the short night. At the Midsomer Fayre the first beams struck upwards rather than down, under the sooted brass rim of the Gallopers' chimney. There was stillness again. The stars of day, those little high birds, reflected music. The trodden grass between the booths turned its blades to take new warmth.

The sun worked round and woke Paul. It came on his face like a pressure. It drove its weight down on to the wooden steps, or lifted the planks against his cheeks. It was hardly possible to tell: what woke him was the ache in his bones.

He sat up and wished he was asleep again. Where he was did not matter, who he was he did not know, what he was he did not sense, in a waking dream of dreaming he was here.

In the listless airs of dawn he heard the churches call four o'clock, one after another, from Avonmouth to Clifton and Bristol beyond, and further, perhaps from Keynsham and Bath, Wells and Thornbury. The branches of HEMPSTALL HEMPSTALL HEMPSTALL. All round larks were ringing treble and tenor bells, the tills of daybreak, checking out the night. Then sleep held him again, cramped on the cold step.

He woke fully, and sat with his head in his hands, to see whether the waking would stick. It was towards five o'clock now, but his head was full of the noises of mind and muscles, and all the churches were silent for him. The muscles were sending most messages. His calves were tender to move or touch. An arm had lost its function during the night. But he was awake at last, and stood up.

He walked clumsily, kicking the steps as he went down them. Angela and the other two were asleep, the green of the tent colouring them, and the undimmed sharpness of the sunlight profiling them on the far side of the tent. Paul reached in and brought out the camping gas cooker and the kettle. He lit the busy fussing flame and put the kettle on it. Used gas rose into his throat and made him cough.

Inside the ride Victoria was waking too. The sunlight here had filled the canvas screen and made it radiate light rather than preserve its rays. On the side away from the sun, shadows were not being cast; a soft pervasive light held the radiance over and under, this side of, and beyond, the twin circles of horses.

Above Victoria's face was poised a printless hoof. A flake of gold leaf, penetrated by light, refocussed and relayed it into her eye. She had seen these hoofs from this position before.

She had a waking terror that the horses would begin a mad ride on her at once. She scrambled to her feet, and then leaned on the nearest stiff creature. It seemed to her that one of the boards of the platform had risen with her, rigidly planking her back.

She saw that the horses slept. This was the night-stable of them all now, not their coursing place. She thought about Robin, and her own bed; she thought about Fran and the baby. She thought that perhaps she should go, leave them for ever, a Wendy to the new child, horse-giver, absent companion, far off on a hillside in Wales, lilting Welsh farm boys bringing butter, eggs, sugar, milk, stray kittens, herself lordly, ladily, remote.

['Myself and me alone,' said Granny, 'of beaten gold my throne,' rocking the stick-backed chair.]

Here was gold, and hard wood against ribs. She heard Paul cough beyond the canvas. She went to a join and looked through. He was there boiling a kettle. He was at the limit of her seeing, and she fumbled for glasses before remembering where they were; and that today she began anew, started afresh. There was no more childhood.

She did not feel older, only colder.

Paul looked up and saw her. She here, she was his for now, in a way that nothing else had been. 'Come and have some coffee,' he said in a dawn whisper. 'Bring your blanket; it's cold.'

She responded with a clear immediate smile. To him it was like another sun. To her it was something different. She did not like coffee and never drank it. But that was only through all her childhood. She would drink it now. The smile was the seal on all her vow.

She drank it. It was like a scorched sweet beef soup, but she was to like the taste; it was part of today and of the future that was beginning in it.

'Is it all right for you?' said Paul.

'Lovely,' she said. It rooted coarsely into her.

Tiny Wee came kicking her way out of the tent and strutted about peevish, shorter than her shadow. She wrestled with a biscuit tin and dropped all the biscuits on the grass, the fallen sugar like powdered ice, frost.

'We're all awake now,' said Angela. 'What's the new baby doing? Take an order point, Tiny.'

'That's the littlest one,' said Paul. 'Marion. We used to call her Tiny Wee.'

'We just stopped doing it,' said Angela, acknowledging Paul's authority, not questioning it when he was not questioning himself.

· Marion had her biscuit. Then she wanted a ride on the Gallopers. Paul said No. Martin came out and began to cajole. He looked solemnly at Victoria.

'It's Paul's girlfriend,' said Angela. 'Wendy.'

'Victoria,' said Victoria. 'That's what I am now for ever, and not Vict like they call me at home, or Wendy like I pretended at school, though it is my name as well as Victoria.'

'No riding,' said Paul to the little ones.

'I would like one long ride before I give it up for ever,' said Victoria. She had not been thinking of an instant gallop, but her wish was enough for Paul.

'I'll light the fire while you drink coffee,' he said. 'It might not be out anyway.'

It was out. There was a cloud of ash hanging about before he had finished, and there was a cloud of smoke above the ride, going straight up like a solid thing and then spreading on meeting some layer of a different density. The Welsh Brights smogged the morning sky.

While the others drank coffee or milk Paul took down the canvas screen, folding and stacking the sheets. Angela got up formally, by putting her shoes on, and did her duty of sweeping the platform. All the rubbish went into the middle, where the ash lay, and had water poured on it to prevent fire.

'There won't be any breakfast until somebody gets here,' said Angela. 'We didn't know we would wake so early.'

'We'll have a very long ride,' said Paul. 'Pressure's coming up nicely.'

It took about forty minutes. Paul spent the time going round the horses, checking the iron straps and the swifts and the grease in the lifting mechanism. Then he and the engine were ready.

'We're all mad,' said Angela, unable to be a prefect, allowing Paul to take charge.

'Is it all right to do?' said Victoria. 'He's got it going for me, hasn't he?'

'A long time now,' said Angela. 'But we've done the ride ourselves before, so it's all right; and no one will hear; there's no one for miles.'

'Waltz March,' said Paul.

'Book music,' said Marion. Martin turned a cartwheel coltishly and looked at the sky for a time, to recover, his thick sweet face blank.

Victoria chose a white horse again. Angela stayed beside Marion. The Gallopers started slow; they had the same amplitude but a lower frequency. Paul lifted the speed a little, and they flew almost silently through the air, only the steam engine hissing and clacking a little, thoughtful and deep, a wave almost audible threshing underfoot.

Paul began the Waltz March and the horses danced to time. When all that was at full tempo and pitch he clutched in the dynamo, and put up the lights, and there was the whole spectacle turning before six in the morning, noise, speed, light, smoke, steam.

Victoria did not fall off, did not feel dizzy. She was herself, her new self, modernly full of coffee; she had been out all night, and she was taking her last ride.

Under the horizontal sunlight under the spinning bulbs, on a flashing dashing white horse with a golden pole to cling to, she was pulled out of her ordinary senses by the whirling and the music shouting, bellowing over the Downs.

Then the music died. Paul had no other book ready at the moment. They went on fast and faster without it; and perhaps that was the greater bliss, but would not have been so without the music first.

Paul had some new effect, of a flashing light, she thought. The music came again. Angela came back along the platform and shouted 'Turkish Delight', which was the name of the tune. It was wild, strange, explorers' music, a symphony fit for the new beginnings, the new and last ride out from the old world.

Paul came down from the engine and stood beside her. She put down a hand and held his. It was nature to do so. She wondered what she felt, and noticed it was nothing much.

There was a still neutrality about the place she now was in. She was to set off from here, but it was itself nowhere, where nothing was very much felt, rather than where anything special or remarkable was.

It was chiefly half past six, morning everywhere.

The music ran through and stopped. There was a voice

calling, like a voice waking her from a dream. She thought she would not be woken.

Paul took his hand away, rather suddenly, and went to the middle of the ride. The voice went on calling. 'Vict,' it was saying. 'Vict.' To some people it was still yesterday.

The lights went out, except for a flashing one. The ride slowed and came to a stop. Steam began to blow from the engine in the middle.

The ride was over. But it had served. She had ridden for ever, and there was no journey any more, she was rid of pink mares, furred donkeys, rocking horses, all the trots and galumphs of children, and was ready to walk herself the rest of the way on her own two feet.

The extra flashing lights were from two police cars, the calling voice Robin's. Why the two came together she did not know. But Robin was up there with her now and explaining.

'I'd better have a word with her, Sir,' said a girl prefect in police uniform. 'You are agitated and may distress her.'

'I'm not agitated about her,' said Robin. 'Why should I be? I've got a spare at home.'

'It's not quite a time for jokes,' said the policewoman, severely, like Robin talking about such things.

Victoria began to explain that he didn't make jokes. But that sort of explanation did not mean much. Everybody was in trouble, but none of it was taken too seriously.

Angela was the one who grew red in the face, when the tent was looked at in a superior manner by two doubting policemen and the policewoman.

'No, we are not living rough,' she said, displaying authority over girls from a school with a different uniform and rules entirely. 'We have spent the night here to keep an eye on the Gallopers. When we left it to you once all the music books were ripped and the coal was stolen.'

'Welsh Brights,' said Martin, to clinch the matter.

Noise of music had brought the first police car up, and while the crew of it were trying to attract Paul's attention they had noticed Victoria, answering the description of missing Clifton schoolgirl, Victoria Wendy Hempstall. Another car had brought Robin up at once. Here they were, wanting to know what had happened, giving order points as if they were sweets.

'Like a skinned rabbit,' Robin was saying.

'Will he grow fur?' said Victoria. 'When can I see him?'

'Fur?' said Robin. 'He might grow a moustache one day.'

'I'm glad you're pleased,' said Victoria. 'Is Fran all right?'

'Of course,' said Robin. 'I mean, yes. It isn't really a matter of course, is it? She is very well, and very pleased, and I think we can say of course about that. She sent a message about mint or sage and carrots. I couldn't understand, but she said you would know.'

['Parsley,' Fran had said. 'I can't afford lettuce or a greetings African marigold.']

'Now are you coming home?' said Robin, probably the third time, by his looks.

'Later,' said Victoria, and she climbed down from the horse and gave him a new kind of hug, an equal kind, the kind he would get from an aunt. A bit Wendyish, actually. He liked it.

'I've got a key,' she said. 'This is Paul.'

196

'Well, young man,' said Robin. 'Everything is happening today. I want her down at the Maternity Hospital by two o'clock.'

'Yes,' said Angela, infected with police prefectoriality. 'We can do that. We're used to it at our house.'

'Yes,' said Robin, not quite adding up all these people, but not worrying about it. 'Made a back-up copy,' he muttered.

Then he and the police cars left.

They've stopped thinking about me, Victoria decided. Good.

'Ride again,' said Marion.

'Fire's gone out,' said Paul. 'What time are they bringing something to eat?'

While Paul thought about that, Victoria went on thinking about herself, Fran and Robin. Fran was all right. Nothing changed with her; she did not even need to be worried about, and would have no more need to rush to hospital for secret reasons. She was going to stay the same.

But life was beginning for Robin, and for Adrian, as well as for Victoria herself. There's more than one of me, she thought. One of me will be about. We shall have to bring him up.

I'm full now. What a strange feeling. I've got bigger than myself. I'm growing happier.

She remembered the University refectory, and that it served very good breakfasts on Sunday. So it was natural to go there with Paul.

'I have a lot of money,' he said.

'You go,' said Angela. 'We'll wait here.'

They went down thinking different things, but what they thought, though it was not the same, held them together and lifted them out of joys they had known before.

Paul saw the new day surrounding Victoria. In all other people he saw not themselves but only reflections of how she looked; in all the streets he saw only things that she seemed to light up. All this was new to him. But at the same time, though he looked at her and found her good, he knew that she was not to be his most prized friend. He had further to go than that. This was the way there, that was all; but for the moment everything.

Victoria was more full of her newness, and of the knowledge that she had come to her own senses. In all the joy of her day Paul was a part, but no more than an element. Perhaps we all know no more than that about each other. Or about our different selves.

At the Refectory Paul asked whether they should go in under that severe arch with its dog teeth of ornament.

'You say you are on a course,' said Victoria, fully in charge now, like a prefect. 'If they ask. We are holes in the paper-tape. Robin says tea-bag, but we both don't drink it.'

That school does it to them, Paul thought. This is how Angela is. Or is it just women?

Then he acutely thought of new bread, bright and crusty against his throat.

They carried trays of breakfast unfamiliar: bacon, sausage, tomato, egg, the char of coffee, rasping toast; like the farm, suddenly in the smoke-sweet hall.

Victoria was seized with passion to write a last farewell to time past. With Paul's fragment of inedible chalk they knelt in a sort of prayer to the part of time ahead. On a stone threshold, and already smoothed and smudged by passing feet, as it was entered, Victoria wrote:

DIARY I call this day tomorrow. Now we have all got to here. Omen.